E. Lynn Linton

Sowing the Wind

A Novel: Vol. I.

E. Lynn Linton

Sowing the Wind
A Novel: Vol. I.

ISBN/EAN: 9783337051914

Printed in Europe, USA, Canada, Australia, Japan

Cover: Foto ©Andreas Hilbeck / pixelio.de

More available books at **www.hansebooks.com**

SOWING THE WIND.

A NOVEL.

BY

E. LYNN LINTON,

AUTHOR OF 'LIZZIE LORTON OF GREYRIGG,' ETC.

IN THREE VOLUMES.

VOL. I.

LONDON:

TINSLEY BROTHERS, 18 CATHERINE STREET,

STRAND.

1867.

PRINTED BY J. E. TAYLOR AND CO.,
LITTLE QUEEN STREET, LINCOLN'S INN FIELDS.

INSCRIBED

TO

MY BELOVED BROTHER

AND

LIFE-LONG FRIEND

ARTHUR T. LYNN.

CONTENTS OF VOL. I.

—◆—

SOWING THE WIND.

CHAPTER I.

SMOTHERED IN ROSE-LEAVES.

In a richly-furnished room in Hyde Park Square sat two young people, gravely playing at back-gammon. The board was of ebony and silver; the stakes were dainty bonbons piled up in a filagree gold basket; the young people them-selves were in full evening costume; and the room was white and gold and crimson, with costly ornaments crowding marqueterie tables and gilded *étagères*, marble slabs and buhl sup-ports, carved brackets and enamelled pedestals, wherever there was the possibility of placing

them. It was quite a wilderness of costliness
and ornament; but it was kept from the appear-
ance of frippery, or even of scattered effect, by
the background of the deep red velvet curtains,
and the pure white of the panelled walls.

The two who sat in the midst of all this luxury
were in keeping with their surroundings—young
and beautiful as was befitting; wedded, loving,
and happy. The one was a man of the type
which some call elegant, and others distinguished
—tall, and slightly built, but with shoulders too
narrow and drooping for the firmer kind of
manly beauty, and with a habit of carrying his
head turned over the left shoulder shyly, which
gave him a boyish and retreating expression, as
of one afraid to expose himself—a man who never
stood square, face to face and chest broadside,
but always a little turned edgewise, with one foot
in advance of the other; and the habit was as
expressive as it was instinctive. His face was
a long oval, and of a sallow hue; his hair was
black, and fell in soft locks naturally waved
and carefully arranged; and his eyes were of a

rather metallic brown when they could be seen, but they were generally cast down, and looked up only at intervals and swiftly, like the eyes of some shy beast within its covert, and as if afraid to have it seen that they looked. He wore a small finely-pointed moustache, but else was clean-shaven; and his face had a curiously Spanish expression, but without the Spanish masculinity of look. His hands and feet were small, and his whole character, as expressed by bearing, face, and figure, was that of a refined and careful gentleman of the true Brahmin class, but without either strength or daring.

The other was of a quite different type. She was slightly above the middle height, generously modelled and richly coloured, with large soft eyes of the true Irish blue, and with a profusion of bright golden hair—not hair of the sleek and silky kind, but mutinous hair, that would curl and break from out the triple bands round the well-shaped head in a kind of aureole, wherein the light was caught by each separate spiral thread, and given back in wonderful intensity of lustre;

her skin was clear, and of a low colour—a rich,
creamy white, where the tender little shadows,
passing into the soft fringe of young hair round
the neck and temples, were golden too; her lips
were broad, and of Italian richness in their colour;
she had the loveliest arms and shoulders that ever
woman had, and she had the finely-arched feet
of a thorough-bred; but her hands, though white
and shapely, were a trifle large—like the hands of
all capable women. She wore the same-sized
gloves as did her husband, but her hands were
firmer than his, and with a fuller and broader
palm; his were long and thin and dry and narrow. Indeed there was a general sentiment of
abounding physical life about her that contrasted
strongly with his more languid grace; and the
contrast was a true one, and expressed the difference between them. And yet Aylott St. John
Aylott was the master, and Isola, his wife, knew
no will save his.

Married at seventeen, she had now been five
years a wife; but her state of matronhood had
brought with it little knowledge of the world,

and less experience of life. Her husband was a man who kept no society, and rarely stirred from home. Reserved and shy, he was also proud and sensitive; and haunted by the fear of ridicule, he was studiously cold in manner, and carefully avoided all outward demonstrations. He loved his wife, and he was intensely proud of his family name, and though only the son of a wealthy incumbent and the grandson of a dean, held himself as too far removed from the ordinary middle class to render familiar association, save with the five great professions, possible. The only person he admitted to his table was Richard Norton, the family solicitor; and this was the lowest point to which his pride could stoop. He was of no profession; for as he had inherited his father's property of two thousand a year, judiciously invested, he had no need to work; and as his money was still where his father had placed it, under Richard Norton's superintendence, he had not even the pleasure of managing his own affairs, and seeing his possessions dwindle in the process, as his occupa-

tion. And he had no brothers or sisters to break
up his isolation. True, there had been a sister
once—a poor, misguided child whose sinful folly
had broken her father's heart; but she was dead
now, and her very name and memory seemingly
forgotten. Even Isola did not know the shameful
story of her husband's only sister; he was too
proud to be able to tell even her how the Aylott
ermine had once been stained; and as Harriet
was dead now—had not Richard Norton buried
her only a few months after her flight?—there
was no need to point out her grave, and show
the shadow lying across it. He would talk freely
enough of his mother, whom he just remembered
as one of the loveliest creatures under heaven,
and tell how she died away from home, in the
house of a physician under whose care she had
been placed, and what a terrible day it was when
news of her death came—and freely enough of
his father; but his sister's name was brushed
away from both heart and lips; and had he been
asked now, he would most probably have denied
that he had ever had a sister at all.

His chief reminiscences were of his father, a grave, tender, sorrow-laden man, who was said to have never smiled again after his wife's death. And in truth the sun of Mark Aylott's life went down into the night for ever as they laid that beloved woman in her grave—that woman for whose love he had suffered so much—and more than suffered, God pardon him! Though then close on forty, he took orders and entered the Church, where, as the incumbent of Greythorpe, a poor manufacturing town, he worked hard and faithfully at his post till he died—a week after his daughter's elopement with a travelling circus-rider. All but this last fact St. John would tell Isola again and again; and these were his only family histories.

It would almost seem by the social barrenness of the past as if the world had stood aloof from the Aylott house—and yet for what cause? St. John had never been to school, consequently he had made no friends of his own standing; there were no uncles, aunts, nor cousins, no family connexions anyhow, near or distant, belonging to him ; and when he married Isola Conway, the two young creatures stood alone in the world, without a friend between them to help or mar their happiness.

For Isola was an orphan, without living relations of any degree save one aunt — the sore point of the Conways. This was a Mrs. Osborn, her mother's sister, who had married a scampish, poverty-stricken, atheistic surgeon, and had of course been cut by the whole family. Charles Osborn, M.R.C.S., with his spatulous fingers and loose professional talk, was as little congenial to the dashing gallantry of Captain Conway, his brother-in-law and Isola's father, as he would have been to St. John Aylott himself; consequently, Mrs. Osborn had been tabooed, and, still under the ban, was known to Isola only by name. And Isola's greatest charm in the eyes of her husband was this isolation of circumstance. He was even glad that no children had come to break up the perfect solitude of their home ; had they come, he would have been jealous of them, as so many rivals to himself, and would have never borne to see his wife's attention diverted from him and his pleasures, and their well-being studied instead. Thus he was perfectly content with things as they were, and above all with Isola's want of family ties. The aunt who had married the atheistic surgeon was certainly an ugly branch in the Conway genealogical tree; but as she was out of sight he did not actively resent what was only a disgrace in abeyance, and not an aggressive sore.

During their five years of marriage, St. John had not left Isola's side for half an hour, nor had she ever crossed the threshold alone. If he had by rare chance business in the city, he drove there in the brougham, taking her with him; if she had shopping on hand, he accompanied her, and sat turning over silks and muslins with as much critical interest as herself. Her milliner and her dressmaker knew Mr. Aylott quite as well as they knew his lady, they said, and asked his opinion before consulting hers. And as to Isola herself, it never occurred to her as

possible that she should choose even a pair of
gloves without her husband's sanction, or take
an independent line of thought or action on any
matter whatsoever, from morals to bonnets.
Her husband ruled her life, without a question
of divided authority ever rising between them;
he tricked her out with jewels, loaded her with
rich dresses and costly trinkets, till she scarcely
knew what to do with the finery which no one but
himself ever saw; he filled her home with expensive furniture and rare knicknacks, till it was
oppressive in its completeness, having no future save breakages; he ordered her daily life
as if she had been a child without reason or free
will, and led her to her pleasures and her likings
as to a drill-ground. All as the expression of
his love, and what he thought due from a man's
superior position, but leaving on her a certain
cramped and stifled feeling, as of one struggling
in silken fetters, and smothered under rose-leaves.

His life was a monotonous piece of orderly
conventionalism, and he never felt the repetition
dull. It was a still life; a regular and luxurious

life; a life of quiet voices, of checked laughter, of stately service, of perfect appointments; there was no passion in it, no excitement, no haste, no slovenliness; it was all dress and solitude and well-trained domestic machinery, and the quiet succession of days and hours, with no home events to set things out of order, and with no outside diversion. It was a life which included neither continuous occupation nor social pleasures; it was neither domestic in the way of active management, nor gay in the way of social amusement; it was simply a cloistered life, with a London drawing-room for the cell, and a young married couple for the priest and nun. But it was a life after St. John Aylott's heart, and he would not have exchanged for it any other the world could have given him. It was the life of an English gentleman, he used to say emphatically, and that was the highest point to which God had yet raised humanity;—in his heart he thought, the highest point to which humanity would ever be raised in this world, and the best preparation for the next.

And now the completeness which was so sufficient to the husband was becoming somewhat
barren to Isola. She would stand by the window, looking wearily at the plashing of the win-
ter rain, or as wearily at the waving of the summer trees, and long to be that bright-faced woman hurrying onward in the cutting wind, poorly-
clad and unprotected as she was, but with a purpose, an object, that gave her strength and animation; she would envy the school-girls walking
two and two, and laughing merrily as the girlish
joke flashed from each to each—unformed, childish girls, who knew nothing, and whose lives
had yet to come—but still she envied them,
watching them through the golden bars of her
well-found prison; she pined to follow that
wretched mother home, to take her children,
ragged and half-starved, and feed and clothe
them, as she had read of in certain pleasant books
that made her heart yearn as she read. When
she heard the voices of the little ones next door,
tears would come into her eyes for the emptiness
of the arms that longed to hold a child of her

own to her heart; and even when the rich city
tradesman, their father, brought home his noisy
friends to dinner on Sunday, and they sat out on
the balcony smoking and laughing, she envied
even them, and wished that she was the friend of
that loud-voiced, merry woman who sat among
them, rubicund and ample in her shining silks,
and seemed to enjoy their jokes and rejoice as
much as they. She longed she knew not for
what, and felt an indefinable oppression she
could not understand. She seemed to herself
like one of the Arabian Nights' princesses shut
up in a brazen tower, where were all sweet fruits
and rich apparel — where was all that girlish
heart could desire—save what? Not the prince;
she had found him, and so far was better off than
the princess in the brazen tower waiting for
him. What was it then she wanted? Married to
a husband who adored her, and who was handsome, young, well-bred, and rich—what was
wanting to complete her happiness? Ought she
not to feel that her life was closed, and that she
had no right to demand a wider horizon?

Nevertheless, these objectless, luxurious days of hers weighed on her like imprisonment or spiritual death; and her soul cried out for the freer air of human sympathy and work, of even suffering, as a relief from the cloying sweetness of the present time. Yet all this sense of emptiness and oppression was buried in the innermost depths of her heart, and no one knew that she was not as content as all men said she ought to be. Least of all had St. John Aylott any suspicion that the idol he had set up in his drawing-room altar was yearning for aught beyond the incense of his love, the richness of his offerings, the safety, seclusion, and luxury of the shrine in which he had confined her. Had he known it, he would have mourned for her as for one on the broad way of inevitable destruction, and would have taken it as meaning weariness of himself only, and as the death-song of both love and happiness for all time to come. She did well, then, to keep back in the silence of her own soul, scarcely confessing to herself, the weariness of her days; she did well even to preach false

words of peace to herself, and to assure herself
again and again, as she did, that she was quite
happy, quite content, asking nothing more than
what she had of fate or fortune at their kindest—
yearning for nothing nobler than to fill up the
narrow measure of her husband's life, and to sa-
tisfy the pride which did not even ask the world
to witness his triumph. She did well. Things
had not come yet to the point when she might
assert her human rights; and, in the meantime,
she must content herself in her shrine, and be well
pleased at the incense offered.

They were sitting together as usual, on the
evening when this story opens, playing at back-
gammon for dainty bonbons. Luck had been on
Isola's side to-night, and she had already won
three dashing games, when they heard the post-
man's ring, and a letter rattle through the box.
They had just begun their fourth hit—St. John a
little put out at his ill-success—when the servant
brought her a letter. Now a letter to Isola was
as unusual an event as was a visitor. Save cir-
culars announcing sales conducted on high moral

principles, and now and then answers or queries
from ladies respecting servants, few letters of any
kind were dropped into the Aylotts' box; so that
when the machine in plush brought her on the
silver salver a real letter—a letter in a long envelope, and addressed in a fine, thin, pointed
hand—it was an event which made her heart beat
and her cheeks flush, as if she had been a school-
girl receiving her first secret love-note. But the
flush soon faded, and left her face with an almost
scared expression on it, as she continued her
reading.

"Oh, St. John!" she said, when she had finished, "I am afraid you will be so annoyed!"

She handed the letter to him with a pretty look
of loving sorrow, as if she had somehow done
him wrong, and was repentant. He took it and
read it in silence, as she had done.

"I am sorry for it," he said coldly when he had
finished, laying it on the table, and turning away.

"What can I do?" asked Isola anxiously.
"What would you like me to do, St. John?"

"Like!" he repeated a little impatiently, "I

think you know what I should like, Isola; not to see her, of course!"

Isola looked down, troubled. "Would that be right?" she asked in a low voice. "Poor mamma told me that if Mr. Osborn were to die, I was to be sure to be kind to aunt Juliana and cousin Jane, for that they would be very poor, and that I was to help them in every way I could. Ought I to refuse to see her—poor mamma's sister—my only relation?"

"That is just it!" said St. John. "Your relation! Had she not been that, I would not have cared so much for the intrusion. But I cannot bear to think of any one having the right to say you belong to them, however remotely. The charm of our married life will be broken," he added fretfully. "You will be no longer my Isola!"

"Could such a little thing as this make any difference to you?" she said affectionately, rising from her chair and going over to him.

"You may say what you like, Isola, it is a nuisance," he answered, still in an injured tone throwing the dice at random. "You know how much I resent the idea of any intrusion, and how I have liked the entire isolation of your life. And the widow of a low-bred, free-thinking surgeon, too—the one to ruin my house!—such an unworthy association altogether!"

"It would have been worse if he had been alive," put in Isola.

"Worse! it could not be worse," said St. John.

"But what can I do?" she asked again, coming back to the main point, and with her face still troubled and her heart still anxious.

"Do as you like," he answered stiffly, after a moment's pause. "You always do as you like, Isola; I only tell you what I should prefer, and I leave you free to follow out your own inclinations. It is your affair, not mine. I have no such disagreeable connections in my family, I rejoice to say; and it will be long before our happiness is menaced by anything of the kind occurring on *my* side."

He spoke as if seriously displeased, as, indeed,

he was, being one of those with whom annoyance by circumstance takes the form of personal displeasure.

"It is so unexpected," said Isola, partly for want of something else to say.

"It is what I might have looked for, had I not been blind when I married you," he returned coldly.

And Isola saw that no good was to be got by continuing the conversation.

"I will answer her to-morrow," she then said. "We can speak about it again."

"I do not wish to speak about it again," said St. John as coldly as before. "You know exactly what I think and feel about it altogether. It is a mere pretence to say we will speak about it again," petulantly.

Isola did not answer. Her husband had not often been so annoyed as this, and had not often spoken to her so unpleasantly; but whenever his temper had been roused by chance trouble, she had carefully avoided occasion of further annoyance. Yet that was difficult, too; for when he

was cross he was cross throughout, and made it
equally an offence whether she spoke or kept
silence.

"Where are we now?" she said after a short
pause, cheerfully, taking up her dice-box and rat-
tling the dice. "What was your last throw, St.
John? deuce ace?"

"I shall not play any more to-night; the game
is spoiled," said Aylott St. John Aylott, shutting
up the board.

CHAPTER II.

THE THIN END OF THE WEDGE.

"I say, Wyndham, I wish you would look into this for me," said Smith, the editor of the 'Comet,' tossing over a packet and a letter to his 'sub,' a bright-eyed, energetic-looking, rather undersized man, with a profusion of black hair and beard, and a general look of animation and business about him. "The girl writes creditably enough, but not quite up to our mark; but if what she says is true, and she is capable of being pulled into shape, we might give her a review now and then; at all events, you see about it, like a good fellow; I am too much bothered with this Mexican business to look after anything just now."

Harvey Wyndham took the packet and the note. He glanced through the first, saw that it contained a few water-colour sketches and a crude but vigorous article on some small event that had just happened; a better article in substance than what many practised pressmen would have sent in; yet not quite fitted for the leader of a "daily"—certain feminine blunders in political economy running through it, and the whole paper wanting that subtle but telling touch of the practised hand.

"Well?" said Smith after a pause.

"She has good stuff in her, but she wants training," said Harvey.

"Just my idea; but we might make her useful. Have you read her letter?"

"No, I am reading it now."

It was a short note, stating that she, the writer, "was one of the women who had to win her bread by her own exertions, and not only her own bread but her mother's also, her father—a surgeon—having lately died, and left them with only business debts and complications. She had been

tolerably well educated, and could do a great
many things fairly well, but as yet had not found
her speciality, unless perhaps in literature.   She
enclosed this article as a specimen of what she
could do if she was put to it.   Would the editor
of the ' Comet' kindly look it over, and tell her if
it showed any power of composition ?   Of course
she did not expect that it would be accepted and
used out of hand, as she knew that all people
must go through a certain apprenticeship before
they could succeed ; but it might serve as an indication of her capacity, and whether she could
make anything of herself or no.   And would he
glance at the accompanying water-colour sketches,
and tell her in which she seemed most likely to
do best, art or literature ?   She apologized for
asking his advice so freely, but she was quite
alone in the world, save her mother, who was not
a business person, and therefore could not help
her ; so she must fight her way as if she was a
man, and put aside all false shame.   She would
be glad of any advice the editor of the ' Comet '
would give her ; but would he please not recom-

mend her to be a governess ? for she had a horror
of children and hated teaching beyond everything
else, and she would rather go out as a housemaid
than as a governess." The letter was signed
"Jane Osborn" in a large, bold hand, and the
address was in Seymour Street, near Cavendish
Square. N.B.—They had a lot of rooms to let;
the house was a huge gangrel place that was
eating them up, and they could not dispose of the
lease;—did the editor know any one to recom-
mend ? They were very clean and cheap. If he
would not mind putting an advertisement in his
paper, it should be paid for honestly when she
knew what it was." Again another "J. O.," if
possible more bold and decided than the first.

"What always amuses me in women's letters
is the small bit of individualism and private history so sure to come in with the business," said
Harvey Wyndham, laughing lightly. "And then
the naïve way in which they ask for favours that
cost both time and money ! the utterly unconscious habit they have of levying black-mail, and
never saying 'thank you' when they have got it !"

"Ah, poor things! they are awfully ignorant of business," said Smith compassionately. "But we'll put in the advertisement for her, and not charge her. What are the sketches like? You are a better judge of those things, Wyndham, than I. You were a brother of the brush once yourself, weren't you?"

"Yes!" he laughed. "I have been pretty well everything in my time."

"A kind of handy man to art and literature, hey?"

"About that, Smith; and no master yet!"

"Well! what are those sketches like?"

"Like her writing—clever and vigorous, but unpractised. She has plenty of go in her, and with a little rubbing up will do."

"Can you go and look after her?"

"Yes," said Harvey; "I can judge better by seeing her. I'll go in a day or two—when I've written my books clear. I say, Smith, how do you find this employment of women answer in the office?"

"Pretty well when they have common sense,

which is not often," said Smith. "Their two
worst faults are looseness and partiality; and
their most annoying, the uncertainty of their
work and their want of reliable power. One day
they do magnificently, and you think you have
found a treasure; the next, they send you in a
dozen slips of trash you cannot use, though you
reserved the subject specially for them, and
threw over a better man who was sure to have
done his work at least creditably. And that
makes them awkward to trust."

"Very," said Harvey laconically.

"Then they are so desperately touchy!" continued Smith in an injured tone. "If you pull
them up for their faults, and rap their knuckles
as you would a man's, they fire up and stand
upon their dignity as 'ladies'—the little fools!
The fact is, the creatures want the cream of both
states — the independence and money-getting
power of men, and the conventional respect of
drawing-room ladies: which is ridiculous, you
know, and can't be done."

"Then why do you have them?" asked Harvey.

He was a quick worker himself, and always grudged the giving away of work which he felt he could have done as well as another.

"Why? Because they do better than men in some things—their perceptions are finer; and because I pity them so much, poor creatures! Such a mass of unprotected females as we have now! They must live, you know; and if they have not men to work for them, they must work for themselves."

"Ship them off to the colonies; organize a large middle-class female emigration. That is the only remedy," said Harvey.

"Maybe; but in the meantime they must live, as I said before; and as some of them can write, I like to give them a lift when I can. They do well enough when under control, but they want a master always. They pay, you know, on the whole; but I confess they are a deal of bother."

"So I should think," said the ' sub ' philosophically.

And then they both laughed, and took up the

tangled ends of the Mexican matter, just then
the most exciting question of the day.

Shortly after this, Harvey Wyndham went to
the address in Seymour Street indicated by Jane
Osborn. He knocked at the door, and following the sickly-looking servant-girl upstairs, was
ushered into the large, comfortless, half-furnished
"first-floor front," which a card in the window
told was to let. Two people were in the room
as he entered. One was a pretty, fair, faded
woman of middle age, shabbily dressed in what
were meant to be coquettish widow's weeds, with
good features spoiled by an expression of vanity
and weakness, and with manners singularly deli-
cate, but fluttered and without confidence. The
other was a tall, bony girl, of twenty-one or
thereabouts; not so much coarse as strong, not
so much bold as hard. She was decidedly plain;
but she had fine grey eyes, large, deep-set, and
intelligent, and she had a profusion of rich au-
burn hair, which another turn of the scale would
have dyed to red. Her skin was of a duck's-egg
white, fine and soft but covered with freckles;

her nose was blunt and positive; her lips wide, clumsy, and ill-defined; her hands were small and good, but her nails were dirty; and her shoes were down at heel, with the stockings rumpled round her ankles. She was quite as well dressed in material as her mother; but while the one made her shabbiness to be forgotten in her innate elegance and scrupulous neatness, the other conveyed the impression of being in rags. In manner she was familiar and abrupt; in gesture, angular and ungraceful; but her face lighted up with so much intelligence when she spoke, that nothing was seen but the deep-set clear grey eyes, and the waving masses of red gold hair, looped in such a grand framework round her well-shaped head. Mother and daughter made a strong contrast as they stood together by the window, and Harvey, looking at the powerful, purpose-like face of the younger, repeated to himself his first dictum to Smith, " She'll do."

" You have called about the rooms, sir ?" said Mrs. Osborn in her clear, finely-toned voice interrogatively.

" No; about Miss Osborn's writings," answered Harvey pleasantly.

" I thought so," said the younger lady in an abrupt manner.

" You did ? why ?"—he smiled.

" I don't know; you looked like business, I suppose : I know of no other reason," answered Jane Osborn, in an off-hand kind of way, tossing back her hair.

Harvey looked at her with an expression half of amusement half of interest. He liked her direct tone—"no nonsense about her," he thought; and felt decidedly disposed to befriend her, in spite of his professional dislike to woman's work and professional jealousy of interference in the press. She was a new study to him ; and Harvey Wyndham was always on the look-out for new studies, as part of his stock in trade.

" What can you do ?" he then said as abruptly as herself, taking his tone from her, as he generally did with his company.

" Anything I might be put to," answered Jane.

" That means nothing. The world is deluged with ' general ability,' " said Harvey. " No speciality ?"

" No : how should I ? I want the first start, as every one does ; you men yourselves want it when you begin life, and I only ask for what you have."

" Women generally want a good deal more than men," answered Harvey, remembering what his editor had said, and, as was his wont, airing another's opinions for his own benefit. " They want all sorts of special coaching and bolstering up, and are too sensitive to be reliable workers when all is done."

" I am not a woman of that kind," said Jane contemptuously ; " and I despise the whole idiotic class of womanish women as much as you do."

" My dear !" remonstrated her mother weakly, " you use such strong language !"

" Well, mamma, what of that ? Bad things want strong language to scarify them as they deserve," Jane answered.

" You are ' thorough,' at all events,' " laughed Harvey Wyndham in a tone of approbation.

" I hope so," she said quite gravely. " Whatever I may be, I am no humbug and no coward."

" But you might be more gentle and pretty behaved," suggested Mrs. Osborn a little fretfully.

" Pretty behaved! that's like you, mamma!"
cried Jane with extreme disdain.

" I hope it is, my dear; I hope I never forget
who and what I am, though I did marry your
poor papa, who was only a surgeon, when I
might have had Dr. Bliss, who was a physician,
and Mr. Twamlow, who was a minor canon."
Mrs. Osborn answered with what she meant to
be stately dignity of manner, poor soul!

" Well, mamma, I don't suppose it is very interesting to the gentleman to hear all about our
private concerns and your love affairs when you
were a girl," said Jane impertinently. " He
has come on business, and I dare say his time is
valuable."

" Not at all!" said Harvey good-naturedly.
" On the contrary, I should like to know all
about you, from first to last."

" There is nothing to tell, and nothing that

any one can know," broke in Jane hurriedly, as if to prevent her mother from speaking. " Certainly nothing romantic in any way ! My father was a general practitioner—"

" A medical man; he was M.R.C.S.," interrupted the mother.

" Osborn, surgeon," reiterated Jane stolidly. " He died about six months ago, leaving us very badly off. We have the lease of the house, and that is all we have ; and we let it out in apartments, as you see—but that is very precarious and we have already made bad debts. So you see I must do something for our living—mamma cannot."

" I wish I could !" said Mrs. Osborn, with an artificial sigh wonderfully eloquent in its way. " But I was brought up so differently ! Of course as girls my sister and I were never allowed to do anything for ourselves ; and when I married as I did"—another sigh—" poor dear Mr. Osborn was in very good circumstances, and insisted in keeping me as I had been used to be kept. So I never had·any opportunity of learning to be practical and useful; and I have not my daughter's strength of character, which would enable me to turn my hand to anything, whether lady-like or not."

" No, you are not much alike," said Harvey, looking from one to the other. ·

" We should be in the Queen's Bench next week if we were," Jane said composedly.

" And if you had not me to keep you up to something like lady-like habits, we should be worse off than even in the Queen's Bench, let me tell you, Jane!" returned Mrs. Osborn sharply, —a timid look of mingled fear and apology crossing her face immediately after. And that look, and the few sentences preceding it, gave Harvey the key of the whole domestic situation.

" That is just as it should be!" he said. " There is nothing like good contrasts to work well. You see the one supplies the wants of the other, and so the wheel goes round."

" I must say I should like it better if Jane was more like me, or even poor Theodora," said Mrs. Osborn plaintively.

"And who is Theodora, if I may ask?" said
Harvey.

"My sister!" sighed Mrs. Osborn—"was, I
ought rather to have said—for, alas! she died
about ten years ago, leaving a sweet little girl
that my aunt Conway brought up. And her
husband died too. He was our cousin, so my
sister kept her name. It is a good name, is it
not—Conway?" with a lingering accent of pride in
her voice; "Osborn is not a bad name either,
though it is Osborn without the e, I am sorry to
say," she continued. "My dear husband, though
not in the highest walks of his profession, was of
a good branch; the younger branch certainly;
but of good blood all the same."

"Not so good as the Conways," said Harvey
at a hazard.

She simpered, smiled, and sighed. "No,"
she said, looking down, "certainly not so good.
You see I married beneath myself, sir. Poor Mr.
Osborn was not my equal in station, and my
family never forgave me; but he was so handsome!—so like Lord George Granville! They

were as like as twin brothers, only that Mr. Osborn was the handsomest."

"Pompey and Cæsar," said Harvey laughing.

"Quite so—that was just it—as like as Pompey and Cæsar," replied Mrs. Osborn fervently.

Jane gave an impatient snort. "What rubbish!" she said disdainfully.

"My niece is very well married," continued Mrs. Osborn, who had not heard the remark. "She married young Mr. Aylott, son of the rector of Greythorpe and grandson of the dean of Chatham."

"What! that puppy St. John Aylott?" cried Harvey.

"Do you know him?" Mrs. Osborn asked in astonishment.

"Not personally, I am glad to say; but my father was once mixed up in some business matter with old Aylott—I forget what it was now —and I have seen this St. John once or twice. I heard that he married not long after the rector's death, and that his wife was a very beautiful girl. Richard Norton, my lawyer and theirs, told me so. And so she is your niece, is she? Do you see her often?"

Mrs. Osborn shook her head. "No," she said pathetically, "I do not know her."

"No? why don't you hunt her up then? She might be useful to you if you want help. They are as rich as Jews," said Harvey Wyndham with astonishment.

"We don't want her help," said Jane very hastily. "I prefer to work for myself, and to be under obligations to no one. I hate all the tribe of rich relations, turning up their noses at poor cousins, and being insolent or patronizing as they are in the humour. I hate the whole kind of thing, and with my consent we will never go into it."

"Pardon me, but that is not spoken with the good sense or business-like way of looking at things that I should have expected from you," said Harvey very quietly. "These are the heroics of a school-girl, not the rational calculations of a woman of business."

"Why, what would you have us do?—fawn

and beg, and be thankful for scraps?" cried Jane vehemently. "Is giving up one's self-respect for a little advantage good business faculty, I should like to know? and trusting to charity, and not to oneself, the best way of getting on in life? If it is, I would rather not have anything to do with it, and I'd rather not get on at all."

"Gently, gently, Miss Osborn! Now you are losing your temper; which is quite an unnecessary proceeding, and one not very flattering to your strength of mind. Only weak people are soon moved to anger, remember." Harvey spoke with imperturbable good-humour, and in the tone of a master giving a lesson to his pupil.

"There, Jane, how often I have said the same thing to you!" cried Mrs. Osborn triumphantly. "Now you see how right I am, and how much to blame you are."

Jane shook back her magnificent untidy hair and laughed. "You are right," she said pleasantly, "and I was wrong; but I was not so cross as I seemed, I was only vehement."

"Vehement! you are always vehement," said her mother pettishly.

"Well, mamma, I believe I am; but I don't mean to be savage. It is only a bad way I have; and you, of all people, ought to know that it means nothing," Jane answered.

And Harvey, holding out his hand to her, said, by way of coping to the little episode, "Now I have no fear of you, Miss Osborn. A woman who can bear to hear the truth is sure to do. You are educable, and that is all we want."

"It depends on who tells the truth, and what it is like when it is told," said Jane philosophically. "And now, if you please, will you tell me what I can do? I suppose you come from the editor of the 'Comet,' if you are not the editor himself."

"No, I am not," interrupted Harvey; "I wish I was."

"Well then, you come from him; so please to tell me—am I to do anything for the paper?"

"Yes," said Harvey, "if you work well and don't blunder. You shall have a batch of re-

views to do for us, first of all. You must feel
your way you know at first, and if you do well,
you will get better things in time."

"I'll do my best," said Jane sturdily.

"All right then! I'll see and send the books
off to-morrow; and," laughing, "don't forget
my advice about the Aylotts. One never knows,
you know; and angels are often entertained un-
awares."

"I shall follow it, most decidedly," said Mrs.
Osborn.

"And you?" he turned to Jane, the smile still
on his bright and animated face.

"If mamma goes, that will be enough," she
answered.

"Yes, my dear," said Mrs. Osborn drily, settling her crape cuff; "perhaps, as you say, I had
better make the first visit alone. I know the
usages a little better than you do; besides, you
will be occupied at home."

"You are quite welcome, mamma, I am sure!"
returned the young lady shortly. "I suspect that
will always be the division of labour between us

—bread-winning for me, and visiting fine folk for you; and I don't envy you your share."

"Then we don't envy each other, my dear," said Mrs. Osborn quietly.

Harvey rose to go.

"I am glad I have seen you !" he said to Jane in that cheery tone of his, which sounded so assuring—and the sentiment of professional fraternity beaming from his face. "We'll see you through, never fear! and, take my word for it, you'll do." He said this as if he had promised her a thousand a year, and was going now to prepare the transfer deeds. "Good morning to you; I hope to see you again soon, and to be good friends into the bargain. We are fellow-workers, you know, so we ought to be good friends, oughtn't we ?"

"Good morning, and thank you," returned Jane. And at that moment she looked almost handsome, her face was so full of hope and the strength which comes from pleasant thoughts. "But what is your name all this time ?" she then asked abruptly. "The girl only said 'a gentleman,' and you have not told us, remember."

"Harvey Wyndham," he answered, "sub-editor of the 'Comet.' Here, if you want to write to me, there's my club," and he laid a card on the table with "Mr. Harvey Wyndham, the Johnson," engraved on it.

"Thank you, I'll write to you at the 'Johnson' then, if I want your advice about anything," said Jane, as if she had known him a dozen years at least.

"Do so, and I promise to answer," he laughed; and, still laughing, shook hands with both the ladies and left the room.

"My dear, are you not very familiar?" asked Mrs. Osborn with fretful timidity when Harvey had fairly gone. "In my time, when I was a young girl, we should not have dreamt of such sudden friendships, and with quite a stranger too! Write to him at his club! it is really improper, Jane!—really improper! I did not like to check you before him, because I never like to say anything disagreeable to you, but

I was shocked at your familiarity; I must say I was."

"I was not familiar, mamma," said Jane; "when one has business to do with men, one cannot be like a little school-girl, or a fine lady either; one must go to the point, and not pretend to be shy or bashful or anything like that. It is too absurd," contemptuously.

"Well, my dear, I know that you will have your own way, so it is of no use talking," said Mrs. Osborn sighing. "I only wish that you would be more guided by me than you are, and not think yourself better able to judge of everything than I am. It would save your poor mamma some trouble, Jane, and yourself a few mistakes perhaps."

"Mamma, I cannot be everything," Jane said seriously. "If I have to work for you and take care of you, I must do it in my own way, and not be a mere machine guided by you or any one else. I let you do as you like, and you must let me do as I like. You go to see this Mrs. Aylott of yours, and I stay at home to write

for the 'Comet,' and surely that is a fair bargain."

"Oh yes!—by the by, my niece. I will write
to her first, I think," cried Mrs. Osborn : she
was easily diverted in her current of thought.
"I will write and tell her that I shall come and
call on her some day soon—that will be the best
way, don't you think so, Janey ?"

"If you like, mamma," was the indifferent
answer.

"But what do *you* think best, Jane ?" asked
her mother anxiously. For all her querulous assumption of authority, she would not have dared
lift her finger against her daughter's prohibition,
and always waited for her permission before she
finally undertook anything.

"You know what I feel about it, mamma. I
hate the whole kind of thing from first to last.
But I may be wrong. Mr. Wyndham says I am
and he knows the world better than I do."

"Then you think I had better write ?" reiterated Mrs. Osborn.

"Just as you like yourself, mamma," said Jane

more courteously than usual. "Do as you like best; it is quite a thing for you alone to decide, and I won't interfere in any way."

"Then I'll go and write at once," said Mrs. Osborn, considerably relieved.

Which was the way in whereby came about that Isola Aylott received a note from her unknown aunt Juliana, widow of Charles Osborn, M.R.C.S., announcing her widowhood, hinting at her poverty, and expressing her intention of calling at 200, Hyde Park Square, at some very early date—the adverb underlined. The note concluded with her daughter's love to her cousin Isola, and her own kind regards to her nephew Mr. St. John Aylott, whose acquaintance she was really quite anxious to make—she had heard so much that was good of him. If Jane had seen that little piece of gratuitous flattery, there would have been hot work that night in Seymour Street, Cavendish Square.

CHAPTER III.

THE WIDOW OF CHARLES OSBORN, M.R.C.S.

IT was just one o'clock. St. John Aylott was
finishing the City article, always the last portion
of his morning's intellectual exercise; and Isola,
apparently absorbed in the mysteries of a bead-
work pomegranate, was thinking of the note to
be written to that unlucky aunt of hers, and what
should she say?

For herself she ardently desired to see her—
the only one who could speak to her of her beloved mother—the only one who had known her
father, and who could tell her whether the minia-
ture worn as a bracelet clasp was like him or no,
and how he stood and looked and walked and
spoke, when young and beautiful like an Apollo,

and before that horrid accident maimed him for life ; and then the cousin, so nearly her own age —only a year between them—why, they might be like sisters together if they suited : as they would be sure to do, thought Isola yearningly. Had she been even surrounded by friends, it would have been only natural that she should have wished to see these relatives of hers, but as things were, her heart turned towards them with an almost painful longing of girlish need for womanly love. And yet she was going to decline aunt Juliana's visit. St. John had been cold and displeased with her ever since the note of yesterday evening, and she had been accustomed to live so entirely for his pleasure that it came to her as a matter of course to refuse the thing which lay nearest to her heart, because he disliked it. She was only thinking now how most tenderly to word her letter, that the pain of her denial might be softened.

Yet what a difficult task it was ! She had promised her mother to befriend this poor sister if ever the time came when she should need befriend-

ing; and the time had come now—but her promise? If she could have helped her with money,
that would have been something; but she did not
hold her own little fortune, inherited from her
mother and therefore almost due, according to
her ideas, to aunt Juliana. It was one of St.
John's fancies that she should not possess a purse
and that she should owe everything to him; and
she had not troubled herself about it until now.
Sometimes she had wished that she could have
given a shilling to some wretched creature selling
battered flowers at the carriage window, or to some
pale, shivering child, looking with longing eyes
at the happy little ones feasting in the confec-
tioners'; but that was all: now, however, she felt
inclined to question her husband's right to with-
hold her income, when she could have made such
good and loving use of it. And this dissatisfac-
tion was of itself almost a revolution in the young
wife's heart; the first time as it was that she
had put into intelligible form the fact that her
married life possessed a flaw, and that she had
cause of grief against her husband.

While thinking thus, full of trouble at the task before her—full of trouble too at St. John's uncomfortable coldness—the visitors' bell rang sharply, and soon after the footman opened the drawing-room door, saying, " A lady wants to see you, ma'am."

Before Isola could speak, a fair-faced middle-aged woman, dressed in widow's mourning, entered the room—a woman tripping, conscious, simpering, coquettish—aunt Juliana herself, storming the citadel and mistress of the situation, through weakness rather than through courage.

Coming up to Isola, she held out a small tightly-gloved hand, saying in a mincing tone, yet honestly moved for all its affectation, " What! is this my niece ?—is this poor Theodora's little Isola ? My dear child, I am so glad to see you— so very glad!" she repeated, giving both her hands now to intensify her pleasure; and standing on tiptoe, she leaned forward and kissed her, catching just the edge of Isola's chin.

" Dear aunt Juliana!" cried Isola startled out of both doubt and fear; and holding the faded little woman in her round firm arms, she returned the kiss with girlish warmth and a strange and sudden outflow of family feeling.

"And this is the husband!" then said Mrs. Osborn, turning to St. John who had risen as she entered, and now stood coldly and stiffly by the window, half turned away. But Mrs. Osborn did not seem to notice his glacial aspect; or if she saw it, then not to regard it.

Fluttering up to him with her best company manners and in her most graceful attitude—her head bent so that her pale blue eyes might be raised with that half-bashful, half-coquettish look for which she had been so often praised when a girl, her lips open and smiling, and the tips of her fingers delicately spread and pushing back her hair—she offered her hand quite pleasantly, indeed almost a little patronizingly; and Aylott St. John Aylott, proud, sensitive, exclusive as he was, found himself compelled to shake hands with, and thus in a manner welcome to his house, his wife's unlucky aunt, the widow of Charles Osborn, the coarse free-thinking surgeon. It cost him an effort; but he did it; for though proud and conventional to an irrational point, he was a gentleman, and understood the force of a gentleman's obligations.

"I am so glad to see you, dear Mr. Aylott!— my nephew as you must let me call you," said Mrs. Osborn, with what she meant to be a pretty air of youthful enthusiasm.

"Thank you," said St. John coldly.

He did not say that he was glad to see her; but Isola, going up to her and putting her arm round her again, said affectionately, "And we are very glad to see you, dear aunt Juliana— very, very glad!"

"Bless you for that, dear!" said the little woman with less than her usual affectation. "And you are so like my poor Theodora!" she added, beginning to cry. "I declare it has quite upset me, seeing you! I was so fond of your dear mamma! We were more than sisters—twin cherries on one stalk—and you are so like her! it brings it all back to me again—all these long years—and all that has happened too; and I so

E 2

cut off from every one, and I am sure, for no
fault of poor Mr. Osborn's; and now they are all
dead and gone but you and me!"

And then breaking down entirely, she turned
away and sobbed.

"Don't cry, dear aunt! you will make yourself
ill!" was Isola's rudderless word of comfort, as
she bent over the poor creature sobbing for the
results of that great life's mistake of hers; but
St. John frowned heavily, devoutly wishing that
Osborn, surgeon, was alive again, to be still the
effectual barrier between Seymour Street and Hyde
Park Square, or that in going to his long home
he had taken his wife with him as his companion.

For the first time since their marriage Isola
was not alive to his displeasure. Though at no
time tearfully disposed, like so many women, and
though a fit of weeping was a thing as rare to
her as to a man, yet her eye-lashes were wet now
as she caressed her aunt tenderly. It seemed as
if she held part of the dear lost mother in her
arms—as if the grave had opened, and she stood
face to face with the dead newly risen. Though

so utterly unlike in character and feature too, there was the usual subtle family likeness—that undefinable something in the voice and the smile and the unconscious gesture of the hand and the turn of the head, that reminded Isola strongly, she scarcely knew how or where, of her mother; and it would have seemed to her as if she was offering an indignity to that mother's self, had she treated this her representative with coldness or disdain.   It is such a strange sensation, that of seeing for the first time one who has belonged to the dead beloved !   Though but the echo of the song—the reflection of the glory— yet has it the ring of the master chord, and the sheen of the living light; if not the dear mother's self, yet it is one who was as her second self— who knew her in her beauty, and to whom she is as present to-day as if it was only an hour ago when last parted with.   And when Isola held Mrs. Osborn to her heart, it was as much the mother as the aunt that she caressed, as much the dead past as the breathing present that she clasped.

Mrs. Osborn's deeper feelings were never of

long continuance. Drying her eyes, and pushing back her scanty blonde hair, which she still
wore in feathery straw-coloured ringlets, she
looked up into Isola's warm and noble face
bending over her, with a quiver of lightsome vanity passing over her own.

"You see what a young thing your aunt is
still!" she said simpering. "I often say to my
daughter, 'Jane, I shall never be as old as you
are.' And I never shall, my dear; for Jane is so
staid and wise!—so strong! quite a strong-minded
woman, as one may say—and I am just like a girl
yet. My heart is as young as ever—a thing of
beauty, you know! and I don't think I shall
ever live to be an old woman," laughing lightly,
"no more than the birds, my dear."

"You are very sweet as you are," said Isola
tenderly; while St. John, with almost a spasm
passing over his handsome Spanish-looking face,
lowered his head and occupied himself by folding
the edges of the 'Times' with mathematical ac-
curacy.

"You dear little girl! you will quite spoil your

aunt," said Mrs. Osborn. "It is very long now
since I heard a compliment on myself. I used
to have plenty, I can tell you; but poor Mr. Osborn was not a man of that kind, and Jane
takes more after her poor papa than me. She is
an Osborn, not a Conway. Now you are a Conway, Isola; and so like poor Theodora!—though
she was short and dark, and you are tall and
fair. You are like your papa too—poor Archibald!—such a handsome man as he was! I remember when we first met him as if it was only
yesterday, and Theodora's petticoat half a yard
below her dress, and she all blushes and confusion and wanting to run away; but I held her
tight, and cousin Archibald walked back with
poor papa to Browbridge, and Theodora and I
pinned up the petticoat behind their backs."

"And then they married?" said Isola, as her
aunt paused for a full stop and breath.

"Yes, and then they married: not all at once
you know, dear, because they had to make love
and all that, and we had to get the wedding-
dresses; but then they married certainly, and a

year after I married too; but cousin Archibald
never liked poor dear Mr. Osborn, and he certainly was very cool to him, though Mr. Osborn
was the handsomest of the two, all except his
hands; and his hands were not good, decidedly;
though he could set a broken leg as well as Lis-
ton, I have often heard him say; and draw teeth
like an angel. ' And you have a handsome husband too, my dear, as well as your poor mamma
and me," she continued, looking at St. John;
"and what a lovely home!" gazing round the
room. " What exquisite taste in everything!
just like poor Theodora and me! Theodora had
especial good taste, the dear love! and did everything well. And I see you have inherited the
Conway faculty, my dear."

"No indeed, all this is St. John's taste,"
said Isola hastily, " I had nothing to do with it.
It was all done when I came to it five years ago."

" Had you not better give Mrs. Osborn a
detailed account of every separate piece of furniture?" said St. John with a forced laugh.

" Then there are two of you with taste," cried

the little woman briskly, "for I am certain you
have good taste, Isola; you cannot be poor Theodora's child else. Your name was her choice—
Isola—such a sweet name I think! so romantic
and uncommon. Don't you think it a beautiful
name, Mr. St. John?"

"Rather," said St. John curtly.

"Rather!" laughed Isola, holding up her
hand to him; but he did not take it.

He was never a demonstrative man, and not
very good-tempered under trials, and just now
he was grievously annoyed, and all the more so,
as he did not know how to help himself out of
his difficulty. It was not as if aunt Juliana had
disgraced herself in any way, so that he might
have a moral as well as a conventional leverage
for her expulsion; if a fool—as she was mani-
festly, thought St. John—she was an honest
woman; and though it is disagreeable to be
associated with fools, yet folly cannot be trans-
lated into a crime, according to the present
condition of society. He wished it could.
There was nothing for him to do, so far as he

could see, but to bear the infliction as well as
might be; but his 'well as might be' did not
exclude the most intense annoyances, which he
showed in his own way.

"Oh, that is very cold praise," said Mrs.
Osborn with what she meant to be a playful
smile, shaking her forefinger at St. John.
"Naughty man! how would you have liked anything so common as Isabel or Sarah instead?
She would have been Sarah or Isabel, I can tell
you, but for Theodora and me, so you know
who you have to thank," laughing. "You were
born on Lago Maggiore, my dear," turning to
Isola; "just think anything so delightful!—and
your dear mamma called you Isola in remembrance of an island there; so you are Isola Bella
by rights. Eesola you know, not Eisola—that's
the way to pronounce it; of course you know
that?—Eesola? Our aunt Conway who brought
you up, your grand-aunt, was dreadfully put out
about it, I remember; and old Mr. Fryer, our
clergyman, would scarcely christen you; but
Theodora and I both stood to it, and we won

the day at last. So there you are, Isola, like no one else, and not Isabel or Sarah, like all the shop girls in London; which is a great mercy," thankfully.

Isola smiled. "I like my name myself," she said, "but I like it best when those I love are pleased with it." She looked at her husband as she spoke, but he, still occupied with folding the 'Times,' did not look at her.

"You dear little thing, how pretty of you!" said Mrs. Osborn simpering. "And yours is a fine name too," she added, speaking to St. John. "Aylott St. John Aylott; so like Sir John, unless people know the exact way of pronouncing it; there are not many better names presented at court, let me tell you. I was quite proud when I read it in the paper, as married to one of us; Isola Conway and Aylott St. John Aylott—I thought them the finest names I had seen anywhere, and was so proud I can't tell you! So was poor dear Mr. Osborn. We had a little party that night in your honour, and you should have heard yourselves toasted!

It was quite pretty the way that poor dear Mr. Osborn spoke of his nephew and niece; he was a good speaker when he warmed up to his subject, and he did warm up to that! I remember poor Mr. Massinger, the artist—he is dead now —he was there too; and we had Canter, the fine tenor you know, and poor Miss Treadaway the Shakespearian reader—she's dead too now, poor thing. Oh, I assure you it was a first-rate party, and Mr. Osborn spoke his very best."

St. John drew himself haughtily away. The idea that *his* marriage had been made the subject of a general practitioner's congratulations, and bandied about in the equality of a joint family history among his low artist companions, hurt his pride as keenly as a blow would have done. Rapid resolutions to leave London, and go down to the remotest corner of England, passed through his brain; he felt as if his whole peace and honour were destroyed—as if his house door had been shattered, and a free way made for all the world to penetrate into the most sacred parts of his home. He who had kept himself so exclusive, so retired, for whose association no one short of the aristocracy or professional dignitaries had been good enough, to be at the mercy of gossips like these—to be discussed and paraded as " my nephew " in the vulgar circle gathered round an atheistical spatulous-fingered surgeon ! It was a terrible trial to his pride, poor fellow ; and if he did not ·bear the ordeal without wincing, we can scarcely wonder at his pain.

After this came some talk of Jane, Mrs. Osborn unwittingly, and by reason of her foolishness, giving a decidedly disagreeable impression of that young person ; bringing into full relief all the hardness and unpleasantness which characterized her, while leaving out of sight the unselfishness and the generosity, the truthfulness and honesty, which would have gained forgiveness for even worse offences than an untidy habit of attire and an unpleasing method of speech.

She did not mean to paint her daughter disagreeably, but incontinence of speech has sometimes the same effect as spitefulness, and miniature-painting of character for the most part por-

trays more blemishes than beauties. Still, she
could not quite obscure that great broad outline
which was so grand in Jane; and for all that
her silliness filled in the details crookedly, Isola
caught enough to make her feel assured that her
cousin, if an original, was neither small nor unworthy, and that she had qualities which would
make her a valuable friend and a not ignoble
adviser. But St. John felt his gorge rise more
and more against both mother and daughter;
and as he sat balancing the paper-knife ab-
stractedly across his finger, thought how he
could best get rid now of this piece of feathery
folly, and how interpose a barrier between her
and Isola which should be effectual for all time
to come. He was more seriously displeased with
his wife than he would have thought possible
half an hour ago; and she—she knew that she
was displeasing him, yet she went on in her ob-
noxious course. Loyalty to the dead mother,
and the strange stirring of her heart for this so
unusual family feeling, proved stronger than her
dread of his annoyance; and despite the anger

which he did not care to conceal, she treated Mrs. Osborn affectionately, and when luncheon was announced, asked her cordially to stay, as she rose and was preparing to curtsey herself away in a shower of coquettish affectations.

And after some little pressing, and a great deal of girlish pretence, aunt Juliana did stay, overjoyed to be once more at a table luxuriously served, and as used to be in her younger days, before Mr. Osborn's handsome face and bold free tongue had lured her into the dingy insufficiency of Seymour Street. And St. John Aylott had to give her his arm and conduct her to the dining-room, as if she had been the gorgeous widow of a duke, and not the shabby relict of a low-class surgeon getting his daily bread out of pills and teeth.

Certainly there was one little point of comfort in this uncomfortable condition of things: Mrs. Osborn was a gentlewoman born, and did not disgrace him before the servants. She was affected and shabby, and her dress had that ineffaceable mark of home-make and clever contrivance which men perceive if they cannot explain; but she was evidently accustomed to the usages, as she said of herself, and understood the etiquette of a well-conducted table. She draped herself in her purple as if it had never been torn or frayed, and drew the folds with conscious grace about her meagre shoulders; and even the wondering servants understood that she " was one of the right sort though she might be a trifle down," and treated her with less than might have been expected of that quiet disrespect always shown to inferior guests in grand houses.

She failed however in one thing—she admired too much; the only sign of disuse that she gave. But she was like a creature long athirst stooping now to drink, and she could not repress her satisfaction. The bed-room, every little ornament and appliance of Isola's dressing-table, the furniture, the service, the dishes, the wines—all were like glimpses of a long-lost world to her, and she could not breathe in the precious airs in silence—she must say to others how precious they were. But her praises irritated St. John as much as any glaring ignorance of forms would have done, and he fretted through the meal as painfully if a real misfortune had befallen him. To have been brought so suddenly face to face with the one deformity of his married life, and to be forced to acknowledge and receive it! Poor St. John! and poor Isola!

When Mrs. Osborn at last fluttered away in a nearly lunatic condition of happiness, Isola went up to her husband somewhat timidly yet very lovingly, and frankly too.

"I hope you are not much vexed," she said. "But I could not help it, dear! Poor mamma's sister! and so like her in some things! And she *is* ladylike, St. John!"

"I will say nothing about it for this once, but it must never happen again," said St. John, turning away.

"What can I do, dear, if she calls again? You heard her say that she would do so," asked the wife anxiously.

"Tell Banks that we are not at home to her for the future," was his answer.

" St. John !"

She lifted her face, flushed and distressed.

"You care more for this mere stranger, seen for the first time, than you do for me?" he said sternly.

"No! no! of course not! but—" she hesitated.

"Well! but what, Isola?

"I should be glad to see her again, dear; I liked her."

"Liked her!" cried St. John with a raised voice; "liked that vain, weak, shabby woman? you liked her, Isola?

" Yes, I know that she is vain and weak too," returned Isola, "but she is affectionate and good-hearted. She is a goose, I admit," smiling; "she always was, I believe, poor darling; but still there is something about her very loveable. And then she is my own—perhaps that is the reason."

"That last argument is unanswerable," said St. John with a sudden spasm at his heart that nearly choked him. "Take your own course now, I will not oppose her coming again. Please yourself, as you always do, Isola ; but do not ask me to approve of what you do, or to say that you do right. Your own!—let her be your own; I of course am nothing ! Now, if you please, we will drop the subject," he added hastily, as Isola was about to speak; " it has lasted too long already."

The drive that afternoon was a silent one. St. John was chafing at this as it seemed to him entire destruction of the special charm which had hitherto distinguished his home; his Isola was no longer his alone—his own solely and wholly ; she was shared like any other wife, with aunts and cousins and a whole tribe of relatives, to warp something of her allegiance, and weaken something of her love. The absoluteness of his possession was at an end, and he saw nothing now before him but a deluge of new affections, of new interests and emotions, which would soon make shipwreck of his home. And then, not being of the nature of those who can hold their own against unpleasant influences, she did seem

less lovely to him to-day for this so unlovely
connection of hers, and as if some of the finest
and sweetest links uniting them were snapped
asunder. And while he was torturing his soul
with thoughts like these, Isola was thinking how
she could best reconcile opposing duties—earnestly desirous to do all that was most pleasing
to her husband, yet anxious not to fail the mother in her aunt; anxious too, to be of some
good use to her in her need, and grateful, in her
spiritual loneliness, for the advent of even so
weak and shallow a nature as poor aunt Juliana's. But she did not want to vex him: how .
then could she be true to both her duties? A
grave problem! weighing down that young head
with its anxious balance, but never coming to
the right adjustment whereby graciousness and
loyalty could be fairly meted out to each.

"Jane, she is charming!" were Mrs. Osborn's
first words when she reached home; "we must
go and see them again very soon; and you must
come next time; we must go very often! She is
an angel, and had the loveliest blue muslin I ever

saw. I tried to carry the pattern in my eye, but I am afraid I cannot manage it, else I would make one for you out of that black alpaca of mine—you know which I mean? She was so sweet and kind that I dare say she would let me have the pattern if I asked; but I did not like to, you know, only the first time of going; and her husband a rather stand-off kind of person I must say, though so handsome, and with a very elegant figure and a sweet little moustache."

"I am glad that you are pleased, mamma," was Jane's tranquil rejoinder; "so they did not snub you after all?"

"Snub me? what do you mean, Jane? and where ever did you hear such vulgar language? I am sure not from me! I never taught you such words, and I can tell you, such expressions as those will not do at your cousins'! And I am sure I hope you will mind what you say when you do go there, else they will think that I am a vulgar creature to have taught you such dreadful things! Snub me, indeed! I should think not!

They were kinder to me than *you* often are,
Jane! Ladies and gentlemen don't snub, as
you call it. And such a house as they have! It
was like old times to see all those lovely things;
and such a luncheon!—and madeira!—just like
the Browbridge madeira that poor papa used to
give us on birthdays. Ah!" with that peculiar
sigh of satisfaction which tells so much, "I *have*
enjoyed myself to-day!—thoroughly! And what
have you been doing, hey?"

"I? I have been reading a stupid novel that
has been sent me to review. Such trash as it is!
But that does not signify. I may cut it up, so I
don't care. Oh! and I have been doing something
else. I have let the second floor back."

"And not the drawing-room?" in a tone of
disappointment.

"I said the second floor back," repeated Jane,
giving a slight sniff.

"Well! that is better than nothing," said
Mrs. Osborn with apologetic briskness; "and
you are a dear good Jeannette, whatever you have
done. Who is it to? Mr. Wyndham?"

"No," said Jane in a peculiarly stolid tone of voice.

"I thought it not unlikely. He seemed to be quite taken with you, Jane ; and now these books," said Mrs. Osborn friskily.

"Mamma ! how can you talk such rubbish !" was Jane's contemptuous remark ; " it is to no gentleman at all, but to a lady just returned from America."

"From America ? Oh dear ! Jane, I hope she will pay her rent all right ! I hope you had some references with her ?"

"Yes, Mr. Richard Norton, Lincoln's Inn Fields," said Jane.

"Richard Norton ! I think I have heard that name before somewhere—dear me ! I am sure I have. I wonder where it can have been, and if poor papa knew him, or what. Can you remember where I must have heard it, Jane ?"

"Yes," said Jane, "Mr. Wyndham mentioned the name yesterday."

"Ah, Miss Jane !" said her mother slyly. Then, seeing the cloud gathering on her daughter's face, she added very hastily, " I think I will go and see this Mr. Norton now. I have my best bonnet on, and I feel a little unsettled. That is the best thing I can do, don't you think so, Jane ?"

" You will be very tired, mamma, knocking about like this," said Jane roughly. She meant it for kindness.

" Oh no, I shan't ! I can take a Bank omnibus, and be put down at Little Turnstile, you know, and that will not give me much walking, don't you see ? I think I had better go and see about it at once," bustling up. "But, by the by," stopping short, "what is her name all this time ?"

" Mrs. H. Grant," said Jane, reading from a card.

" Give it me," said Mrs. Osborn.

She looked at it and read the name, with " Mr. Richard Norton " written at the top in the same handwriting as the card itself. Turning it over, according to the restless way she had, she suddenly exclaimed, " Why, here is another name, Jane ! Who's this, I wonder ?"

" What is it, mamma ?" asked Jane indifferently.

" Gilbert Holmes," said Mrs. Osborn, " The Travellers' Club."

" Oh, bother !" cried Jane, " Gilbert Holmes is no business of ours. Some friend of hers, I dare say. She looks just the helpless little idiot to make friends with every one she meets."

" But it is so very odd," returned her mother, " so suspicious, I may say, Jane."

" Leave Gilbert Holmes alone, mamma, and go and see Mr. Norton about the reference, if you are going at all," said Jane authoritatively.

And Mrs. Osborn fussed herself away obediently, saying to herself as she went along, " Poor Jane, what a Turk she is, and how she thinks she manages me !"

CHAPTER IV.

HONOR WILSON'S LEGACY.

RICHARD NORTON was at home. This was one of his peculiarities, and the main cause of his professional success—he was always at home. Go when you would, you found him sitting in his dusty little office, surrounded by papers and ready to give a bland and willing hearing to your trouble. He seemed to have no other life save at that desk of his, and to know no other pleasure than what was to be had in drawing out wills and marriage settlements, and fighting cases through the various law-courts. His whole existence was professional; and from the starched and spotless shirt-collar to the well-fitting and

irreproachable boots—from the first word of quiet
advice "not to go to law if it could be avoided"
to the last shifty turn of sharp practice, he was
the lawyer and the gentleman throughout.

Too much used to evil to affect either horror or
surprise at any manifestation of it that might be
offered, nothing shocked his moral sense, and
nothing moved him to generous anger. He accepted humanity as so many averages, and vice
and crime and knavery as of the inalienable conditions resulting. But he was a kindly-natured
man all the same, and could feel sympathy if not
abhorrence. He was specially kind and helpful
to women, whom he pitied as victims and despised as slaves, and whom he helped to get together an independent income by every means
possible to him, save giving them tangible assis-
tance out of his own pocket. That did not come
into his code of morals anyhow; which at least
had the effect of rendering his good offices less
embarrassing to the recipient. He had always
on hand a stock of distressed females, who cost
him money's worth in time and thought, and for

whom he took real trouble gratuitously; and, good-looking bachelor though he was, and still in the prime of life, unhappy wives, disconsolate widows, and desolate orphans, all flocked to him as naturally as penitents to a confessor; and no one thought it odd, or looked suspiciously on the arrangements.

He was at home now when Mrs. Osborn called, but engaged. "Would she wait? Mr. Norton would not be long," the clerk said, handing her a dusty chair and the supplement of the day's 'Times,' which he seemed to think reading quite lively enough for a client waiting for an audience, and which Mrs. Osborn took patiently, as if it formed part of the natural order of proceeding.

While she was sitting there, conning over the various prices of coals and the excellencies of the Sydenham suits, a dark-haired, well-set, business-like man was talking to Mr. Norton in the inner office—our old friend Harvey Wyndham, just now hampered with an executorship that was giving him no end of trouble, and of which there was one special clause that plagued him like the deuce and all, according to his own manner of expression. So he came to Richard Norton, whom he had employed a year or two ago when one of his publishers had broken some technicality of agreement which "gave him the pull on him," and he thought that a lawsuit would be a fine advertisement for his book, and give it a lift by no means to be despised. And as Norton had pulled him through that with success, he thought he would give him a turn with this, and see what would come of it.

"But the most embarrassing thing of all is a bequest of five hundred pounds to one Honor Wilson or her heirs; and who Honor Wilson is, or where she lives, or how to get at her, I know no more than the man in the moon," said Harvey impatiently, in continuation of his narrative.

"Honor Wilson! indeed!" exclaimed Richard Norton.

"Do you know her?" asked Harvey.

"I once knew a woman of the name of Honor Wilson," returned the lawyer cautiously.

Harvey smiled. "The answer betrays more than it tells," he said lightly.

"You must not be too clever, Mr. Wyndham," said Mr. Norton with unmoved gravity; "you may look through mill-stones, you know."

"You are right," Harvey answered, catching his tone. "It is a way we men of the world have, but it is not a safe one; and, as you say, we get nothing by spending our time in looking into mill-stones and searching for mare's nests. Is Honor Wilson alive now?" he continued in a quiet, matter-of-fact manner, simply addressing himself to the business on hand.

"I have lost sight of her for some years," answered the lawyer; then, as if to prevent further questioning, he took a sheet of paper whereon to make notes, and turned the table on his client dexterously. "Who did you say the testator was?" he asked.

"Massinger, the artist," answered Harvey; "a great friend of mine, though he was an older man by twenty years or so."

"How does he particularize this Honor Wilson?—any profession?—any special indication?"

" No, only of Clipstone Street, Fitzroy Square."

" The date of the will ?"

" Thirty-three years ago."

" Have you made inquiries in Clipstone Street ?"

" Yes, but the people of the house have changed fifty times since then, and I could get no information. One old woman, a neighbour, who was called in as the oldest inhabitant of the quarter, said she thought she remembered the name as that of a 'fine rash' girl who once lodged there. She had something to do with men who paint, the old woman said; and, according to her, was no better than she should be, poor soul."

" Just so," said Richard Norton drily. " Honor Wilson was an artist's model."

" Massinger's ? "

" Yes, Massinger's."

" I understand that accent," Harvey Wyndham said with a little laugh. " Model, and something more I would say ? "

" You are quite right," returned Richard Norton. " She was his model and something more."

" Well, I always suspected that poor Massinger had had something to take the heart out of him somehow," said Harvey. " I suppose it was this girl? It must have been more than a mere *liaison*, as he left her this legacy; and none of his own family knew of any attachment whatever among the confessed relations of society. I should think it was this Honor Wilson?" He looked as if waiting for an answer.

"Most likely," Mr. Norton returned philosophically. " He was madly in love with her, I believe, and when she left him he nearly broke his heart. He was never the same man again, I have understood; but I did not keep up my acquaintance with him, and we drifted quite apart for years before he died; as men do drift in London."

" Did you follow the fortunes of Honor Wilson after she left him? Do you know what became of her?"

" She married," answered Mr. Norton. " Who is the residuary legatee?" he then asked.

" Gilbert Holmes, Massinger's nephew," an-

swered Harvey; "a man out in California, I believe; at all events not to the fore. I have
written to him at his agent's, but hearing nothing, I presume he is still out of the country."

"I know Gilbert Holmes well," said Mr. Norton; "and I think you may count on seeing him
soon."

"Has he returned?" asked the other.

"I cannot answer for that, for I have not seen
him, but I believe he has."

"I will give him the business to do as soon as
he is here," cried Harvey. "He has all the
good of it, and I have not the benefit of a penny-
piece, so he ought to take the trouble. He may
find out this Honor Wilson and release me. It
is going to be no end of a bother, that I can
see."

"Leave the matter in abeyance for a short
time," said Richard Norton. "I dare say I
could trace out this woman," he continued, looking down and drawing figures on his blotting-
paper, "but it will be a work of time, and you
must leave the matter alone for the present. We

cannot hand it over to Gilbert Holmes yet—not
until we have thoroughly satisfied ourselves that
Honor Wilson is dead and has left no heirs,"
here he coughed slightly; "but that will take
time to prove, and for the present leave things
alone."

"I ask nothing better," said Harvey. "My
time is so taken up with my own work that a
thing of this kind is a horrid bore, I can tell you.
I do not see any material in it even," laughing.
"If I saw an article now—or the backbone of a
novel—that would be something; but a mere
piece of troublesome business, with no possibi-
lities in it—" He shrugged his shoulders, but
watched Mr. Norton's face keenly.

"Just so," said Richard Norton, looking up
with a curious glaze over his eyes. "As you say,
if there were materials for a romance, now, in
the history of Honor Wilson and her heirs—"
Here he stopped; his accent made the sentence
complete.

"One is never in want of material," Harvey
answered after a pause; "for what odd things

there are in life ! If we authors were to put into our novels half of what we know to be actual fact, we should have the critics down upon us for ' unnatural incidents,' 'strained effects,' and 'want of truth to nature' generally. We dare not write what we know, and that is the simple truth."

"Just what I am continually saying," said Richard Norton. "Men in my profession hear so much; we of all men know how much stran- ger truth is than fiction."

"And the odd coincidences that come about— the strange lines of relation that cross one at all times! Every one knows something of every- body, and go where we will—meet whom we will—we never get to absolute isolation."

"Very true," said the lawyer rising, to give Harvey a hint that the interview was at an end. These are reflections which every one makes; and as they formed part of the stock-in-trade of the lawyer himself, it was scarcely to be expected that he should be much interested in them from another. Besides, he looked upon Harvey as clever enough in a way, full of pushing business

faculty, which ranked as a moral virtue with
Richard Norton, but flashy and superficial too : in
which perhaps he was not so far out.   Harvey
took the hint, and shaking hands with that warm
and genial shake of his, so peculiarly part of his
dumb language, passed into the outer office,
where Mrs. Osborn was sitting, still occupied
with the supplement of the ' Times.'

"Mr. Wyndham!" cried the widow, in extreme delight at seeing a face she knew.

"Is that you, Mrs. Osborn?   I hope nothing
very serious brings you to our friend here," was
his laughing rejoinder.

"A case in point," said Mr. Norton.   "Here
are two visitors—two chance visitors, as one
may say, of whom one is a stranger"—with a
little bow to Mrs. Osborn—"and whose business
is, I presume, totally foreign to each other, and
yet they are acquainted.   Now, how many diver-
gences did it take to make that coincidence?"

Mr. Norton said this in the tone and manner
of a man probing a really deep and difficult point
of social statics.

" Yes, indeed," simpered Mrs. Osborn; "and I have to thank you, Mr. Wyndham, for another charming coincidence. I followed your advice, you see," flirting her handkerchief.

" What a wonderful woman ! " ejaculated Mr. Norton. " I wish some of my ladies would follow my advice ! "

" And I went to-day, and I have been so happy ! " continued the widow excitedly, while Harvey looked at her in amazement, having totally forgotten the advice to which she referred. " My niece is such a sweet person ! and Mr. Aylott is charming too !"

" Oh, I see !" broke in Mr. Harvey Wyndham.

" But my niece is the dearest creature imaginable ! Such a beauty !—and so like her poor mother ! "

" Aylott? that is not a common name," said Mr. Norton. " What Aylotts are you talking of, pray? The Aylotts of Exeter, or the Aylotts of Newcastle ?"

" Aylott St. John Aylott, son of the incumbent of Greythorpe and grandson of the dean of

Chatham.   He married a Conway—my niece, Isola Conway," said Mrs. Osborn, as if she had been speaking of the alliance of Percies and Plantagenets at the least.   " Do you know them, Mr. Norton?" just a shade condescendingly, her relationship exalting her for the moment.

"Yes, very well.   I am his solicitor," said Mr. Norton with a smile.   " Their business has been in our house for three generations.   I knew the late Mr. Aylott intimately"—with another smile, a little more veiled than the last—"and did all his business for him."

" Was there not something queer about his marriage?" asked Harvey.

" Queer?   In what way?"   Mr. Norton spoke quite naturally, and as if he had never heard a rumour.

" He married some low woman, did he not?—a dressmaker, or cook, or something of that kind? So I remember hearing.   And then his daughter —did she not run off with a groom?   I have only an indistinct recollection, but I know there was some scandal about the old fellow's womankind."

"I don't know what you may have heard,"
said Mr. Norton quietly; "but you have certainly heard very far from the truth if you have
heard any scandal. Mr. Aylott's wife was a perfectly respectable young lady—a remarkably fine
woman, and an honour to any man's establish-
ment; the daughter, poor girl, did make an unfortunate marriage; but she is dead now, and so
that matter is at an end."

"What was the mother's name?" asked Harvey Wyndham; "where did she come from?"

"She was a Miss Fitzwilliam," said Mr. Norton very distinctly, "Harriet Fitzwilliam; and
she came out of Cornwall."

"I am glad you have denied the story," Harvey returned; "for I have always believed it; and
believed too that his unfortunate marriage stood in
the way of the old fellow's preferment. I remember
it being said that he would have been a dignitary
else, for all that he went into the church so late
in life. You know there were not wanting ill-
natured people to say that he took orders as a
kind of penance for his sin in marrying a good-

for-nought—indeed many people said that he never married at all : which I always thought scandal, I must own. Still, the daughter's escapade gave some colour to these reports of the mother's having been loose and odd."

" You see the mistake now," said Mr. Norton.

" Oh, perfectly," answered Harvey.

" I am sure there is nothing odd about my niece and nephew," said Mrs. Osborn. "As charming young people as I have ever seen— quite charming they are ! "

" Can't you introduce me, Norton ? " laughed Harvey Wyndham pleasantly.

The lawyer shook his head. "Young Aylott is a queer fellow about that kind of thing," he said. " He is one of those reserved men who shrink from society of all kinds. A thousand pities, as I often say to him ; but what can be done? A high-spirited young fellow with money and his own master—who has any chance of guiding him against his will ? I wish I could make him see life and his social duties differently. I have done my best, I can assure you."

"What a duffer!" said Harvey pityingly.

"It is a great misfortune for her," Mrs. Osborn said. "She ought to go out everywhere; a beautiful young creature like that ought to go to balls and parties every night; and to all the courts and concerts, and everything. We used to go to everything when we were her age; though to be sure Browbridge was not like London; but then our poor papa had not my nephew's purse."

"Persuade him to take Mrs. Aylott about!" laughed Richard Norton, as if he had given her a riddle to guess.

"I wish I could; I should like to have the pleasure of introducing her," said Mrs. Osborn enthusiastically. "Is she not beautiful, Mr. Norton?"

"Superb!" cried that gentleman with fervour.

"I must positively know her if you go on like this," exclaimed Harvey laughing. "It is cruel! Mrs. Osborn, you must introduce me if Mr. Norton will not."

"Very well, I will," she answered with a flutter of the familiar purple. "I am her aunt and can

surely take such a responsibility as this on myself."

" You are standing all this time, Mrs. Osborn,"
said Mr. Norton, moving towards the inner office.
" Will you not come into my office, and tell me
what I can do for you ?"

" I do not want to take up your time," she answered, with an almost appealing look towards
Harvey Wyndham—she did so desire to go out
of the place with him !—it would be such a pleasure to her to walk once more with a well-dressed,
well-looking man, through the crowded thorough-
fare !   " I have only called to ask if this lady's
reference is correct.   She has offered to take a
spare room we have in Seymour Street—since my
poor husband's death, and not wanting rooms
for the patients and consultations and things, we
have more space than we want ; and as we are
two ladies alone, my daughter and I, and neither
of us very old yet," with a simper, " we are
obliged to be very particular, you see," spread-
ing out her fingers like the Venus di Medici, and
pushing back her hair.

" Who is she?" asked the lawyer, taking the paper from her hand. " Oh! Mrs. H. Grant, is it, from California? My God! and to you," he muttered below his breath. " I see she gives me as a reference," he then said in a matter-of-fact voice, but looking at Mrs. Osborn from under his eyebrows furtively. " Yes, I think I may endorse her; I think I may," reflectively. " Yes; you may trust her for the rent and general propriety, I think. She has just returned from California, has she not?" abruptly.

" Yes, and that made me rather suspicious of her, I must confess. America or California or some place like that—so very odd, you know, for a lady to have gone out there!" said Mrs. Osborn with a look of innocent astonishment, as if it fatigued her even to think of such a thing.

" Talk of coincidences again; look here," said Mr. Norton to Harvey, showing him the name of Gilbert Holmes on the back of the card. " The very man we were speaking of."

" By George, so it is!" cried Harvey. " The Travellers' Club, too?"

" Yes, but his agent's, where you have written, is safe. You will hear from him in a day or two, you may be sure."

" I hope I shall," said Harvey, stretching himself, " and so get rid of this will business. By the by," turning to Mrs. Osborn, " did your daughter get her packet from the office to-day ? I was very careful in sending it early, and choosing what I thought she would like."

Harvey Wyndham understood the value of patronage as well as most people, and knew exactly where it placed him, both to give and receive. And he wanted Richard Norton to think him a social potentiality, for there were sundry bills of his coming due, which he would rather not have to meet single-handed—so he was casting about for a staff of strength, if haply such could be found.

" Yes, thank you, so much, I am sure !" said Mrs. Osborn. " I left her hard at work, poor girl, when I came away. She is a very good girl is Jane—though I am her mother and perhaps ought not to say so—but she is certainly an industrious creature if ever there was one."

"Oh! you need not thank me!" said Harvey pleasantly; "we brethren of the press are bound to help each other, and it is only the duty of us older stagers to give a helping hand to beginners."

"Has this lady a daughter who writes?" put in Richard Norton.

"Yes, a sensible girl, with a capital square head of her own—a girl that will do, if once she gets a fair start," answered Harvey.

"Oh, you are too kind, I am sure!" simpered the mother, "and my daughter thinks so too!" with an arch look that made Richard Norton smile. He knew that special bait so well!

After this there were a few more words, by way of final drainage, and then Harvey, taking his leave, found himself entangled at the door with the fair-faced widow; and for the sake of courtesy and good nature gratified her wish so far as to walk through Lincoln's Inn Fields with her, and put her into an omnibus in Holborn.

" If he would take a fancy to poor Jane !"
thought the widow, ringing the changes on that
thought all the way home, and arriving finally at
the blessed conviction that Harvey Wyndham
and her daughter were made for each other, and
that they would marry and write books together,
when perhaps she would go to the Aylotts' to
live, drink madeira every day for luncheon, and
wear blue muslins like Isola's. But then her
widow's cap ! heigho ! and her forty-three years,
with the latter half spent in bitter servitude to
poverty, and straining to make two wide gaping
ends meet decently together ! Dear ! dear ! what a
pity that she could not be young again !—though
to be sure her poor dear husband used to say
no woman was worth anything till she was forty,
and she was only three years beyond ! Oh ! if
she could only be young again, and redeem the
past in a blue muslin like Isola's !

CHAPTER V.

COUSIN JANE.

St. John Aylott was a difficult person to deal with. He was one of those refined and honourable men whom one must esteem for certain high-class qualities, but whose uneasy tempers and fretfulness under small annoyances make them trying companions to live with, and tax a woman's fidelity of respect sorely. Sensitive and reserved; loving yet undemonstrative; easily wounded but never uncovering his wound—simply withdrawing himself in coldness and silence and leaving others to guess when the shaft had fallen and where it had struck; he was always taking offence at slights existing nowhere save in

his own imagination, or fretting at some want of
loving responsiveness which no one but himself
would have noticed at all, but never coming to a
frank explanation nor making an intelligible complaint. He expected that his inner life should be
discerned without the aid of speech, and that he
should be understood by a kind of mesmeric free-
masonry not necessitating utterance. And he
was hurt and grieved when those with whom he
lived failed in such insight.

Isola had long since learnt these peculiarities
of his; but she accepted them as she accepted
most things—with that calm patience which is
neither the sleepy indifference of the phlegmatic
nor the slavishness of the weak, but which is the
healthy self-command of power and the broad
charity of wisdom. Hitherto their wills had
never come into collision. The obedience which
a young creature of seventeen, already used to
live under domination, would instinctively pay
her husband had not been broken up, and the
girl grew into the woman with all old habits un-
disturbed. It was still absolute authority on the

one hand, and as absolute submission on the other; and if Isola pined for a wider life, she pined dumbly, and no one knew that she felt her bonds hang heavy on her wrists.

This matter of Mrs. Osborn perplexed St. John Aylott as nothing had perplexed him before. He did not know how to act, and he was not the man to seek advice. He did not like to forbid his wife an association where no moral blame attached, but he wished her, of her own free will, to sacrifice her desires to his. Yet he was too proud and reticent to·say this, so took refuge in coldness and unhappiness, according to his wont. And he was unhappy. Small as was the whole burden of his annoyance, yet he suffered as if it had been the ruin of his life, and went about in a state of gloomy misery that made Isola's very heart ache to see. But what could she do? He was her husband truly, and she therefore owed him obedience; but had she no sense of right herself? was the better thing of no account? and ought she to commit a baseness, as it seemed to her, merely out of cowardly fear and to keep him

in good humour? Was it right to give up a
moral principle, simply to please even a husband? Ought she not rather to believe in the
real nobleness underlying this meaner conventionalism, and to act up to the better self now
hidden? These were the thoughts of conscience,
not of self-will; and right or wrong, they affected
her powerfully. They touched the unsolved problem of married life, and uncovered the cancer-
ous sore of home, namely, the right of the woman
to independent moral action in opposition to her
husband's will—her duty to God as represented
by her conscience, or her duty to the social law
as represented by her wifely submission. And
Isola was just beginning to be afloat between
these two great tidal opinions.

Still the matter rested in abeyance. Mrs.
Osborn had not called again in Hyde Park
Square, and Isola had taken no measures to invite or forbid, but sat waiting on chance and the
ordering of events, bearing her husband's varying
moods with an elastic cheerfulness which fretted
him more than the most vehement outburst of

temper would have done. But not understanding fully his perverseness, whether he was peevish or silent, formally polite or coldly dictatorial, she was always the same—patient, affectionate, forbearing—not seeing when he meant to annoy her, and not resenting what he intended should offend. Can a greater wrong be offered to any one who means to be disagreeable and aggressive?

They had not to wait long on chance and the ordering of events. The temptation of going again to the place where she had been so happy for her hour's readmission into a lost elysium, was too strong for Mrs. Osborn to resist. Of those with whom the lessons of bitter experience fade like unfixed photographs in the sunlight, so soon as fortune turns her wheel but half a spoke's length to their favour, she had forgotten now that she had ever married into poverty and social humility, and been ostracized in consequence. She was simply Juliana Conway again —a widow with a daughter of whom she stood in mortal fear—but a Conway all the same, and of equal rights and privileges with the rest; and

the likelihood of Aylott St. John Aylott object-
ing to her society never crossed her poor feather-
brain as possible. Exactly five days then, after
the first visit, and precisely at one o'clock, the
door-bell of 200, Hyde Park Square, was rung
sharply as before, and both Isola and St. John
knew who was standing on the doorstep waiting
for admission. Isola flushed to the very roots of
her hair, while St. John turned white and livid
as the servant flung open the drawing-room door,
announcing "Mrs. and Miss Osborne."

"You dear little thing! you see I have come
again!" said Mrs. Osborn airily. "I could not
keep away any longer; and I have brought
Jane this time, as I said I would. There, Jane,
that is your dear cousin Isola, and so like your
poor aunt Theodora and your uncle Archibald!
and that is your cousin St. John. Mr. St. John,
do you think Jane anything like me, poor dear?"
fluttering up to him and laughing girlishly.

St. John gave one glance to the new cousin
standing in a kind of defiant awkwardness near
the door; only one—he did not care to give a

second, neither did he speak; but Isola, though
also shocked, conventionally, at the untidy red-
gold hair flowing in unruly masses everywhere,
the crumpled dress, the angular action, the
superficial unloveliness of the new comer, went
up to her kindly and said, "I am glad to see you,
cousin Jane," in a bright and cheery voice, cordially, as she did most things. And as she looked
into her freckled face, plain and unattractive as
it was, she felt the strength and honesty that
shone through it, and knew that here was one
whom she could respect and believe in, and
whose influence would be pure and healthy.

Still St. John did not speak. He stood where
he had risen from his easy chair when they
entered, quite silent, with a displeased and
haughty face turned slightly away. Jane walked
straight up to him and offered her hand.

"How do you do, St. John Aylott?" she said
in her harsh abrupt way, quite unconscious that
the ends of her fingers were through her gloves,
and that St. John Aylott would as soon have
touched a reptile as her hand. It was well for

her that she did not see him, immediately after, draw his handkerchief through his fingers as if to wipe off a soil.

"I am afraid we are nuisances," she then said, fixing her eyes on him searchingly.

"Nuisances! no! no!" cried Isola hurriedly, "we are very glad to see you."

Jane made an odd kind of grunt. It was a wordless ejaculation and might mean anything.

"Jane!" said her mother in a low voice, half beseechingly.

"There is nothing I hate more than humbug," said Jane, wheeling round and looking straight into Isola's face. "If one is in the way, why can't people say so, and not pretend that they are glad to see one when all the time they are wishing one at Jericho? If we are in your way now, or your husband's, why on earth not say so, and just send us off for another time!"

"But you are not in the way," repeated Isola; "and even if you were," smiling a little timidly, "would it not be our duty to give up our own pleasure for yours?"

"Not at the expense of truth," said Jane argumentatively. She was one of the women bristling at all times with argumentation, preferring inded any amount of discussion to agreement, liking, as she said, to get to the back of people's minds. "I don't like to hear you uphold humbug, Isola, in any form. You look too honest for that, and I shall never be good friends with you if you give in to it."

She said this quite as if her friendship was worth having; as indeed it was—as is the friendship of every honest soul. But her words grated on St. John, and irritated him almost beyond his power of self-control. Things were going rather too fast, he thought, when Jane Osborn, that rude, unlovely boy-woman, that ill-dressed, crumpled creature standing there, could presume to patronize his wife, and prescribe the tone of thought that alone could ensure her friendship!

"I hope Miss Osborn will find my wife worthy of her kind patronage," he said with a strange flash in his eye. "We can scarcely hope to obtain her friendship," with a sneer.

"Oh ! nothing signifies to me but a person's real worth," Jane answered indifferently—"your wife or a duke's, it is all the same. It is character, not station, that I look at."

"Of course your own moral superiority gives you the right of choosing your friends from all stations," said St. John ironically.

"Ah !" said Jane rubbing her nose, a trick she had at times, "there's not much recognition of moral superiority in that speech. You are mistaken if you think I do not understand you, Mr. St. John."

She spoke without a trace of ill-humour; she only wanted to let him know that she understood him, that was all.

"I do not know what you mean," he said unpleasantly.

"No ?" was her matter-of-fact reply. "I should have thought you would. You look as if you had perception; but looks often deceive one."

"I am sure that you are clever, dear Mr. St. John, very clever indeed !" said Mrs. Osborn flatteringly; then in an undertone, " Jane, I am ashamed of you! how can you be so rude?"

" Don't be absurd, mamma!" retorted Jane aloud, "I am not rude, and you know that I am not!"

" Pray: do not let me be the cause of any dissension between you and your daughter," said St. John, speaking to Mrs. Osborn.

" Oh! mamma and I are always sparring!" cried Jane philosophically. " We are so thoroughly unlike in all things that we never agree for five minutes together. That is nothing new!"

" Well, I do not wish to be the cause of either sparring or disagreeing," said St. John with almost ferocious irony; "and as I should be sorry to be that cause, I will wish you good morning."

He bowed with contemptuous stateliness and passed out; and soon after Isola heard the street door shut hastily, and knew that her husband had left the house alone, for the first time since they married. She felt her face and neck flush

again, but when the first pain was over she was
relieved that he had gone, knowing what he
would have suffered and shown had he remained.
His going, too, left her freer both to feel and
to express; for in spite of his annoyance she
was glad to see the Osborns, all drawbacks
notwithstanding. The strange glory of the mother's likeness still hung round her aunt, rendering her in a manner sacred to Isola, while Jane,
abrupt and rude as she was, was yet so full of
character, so strong and truthful, that she was
like "a bath of life" to the woman stifled by
conventionalities and denied the free use of even
thought. And though she was as disagreeable
as must needs be an earnest, energetic woman,
not pretty in person, nor graceful in manner, nor
conciliatory in speech, nor sympathetic with
artificial woes, yet Isola forgave all her unpleasantness for the sake of her nobleness and
power. What signified an ungainly manner or
an unlovely person compared with truth and
strength? she thought, looking at the blunt-
nosed, freckled face before her with kindly

warmth. And Jane caught the look and said to herself, " She is worth saving." Without know- ing why, she felt there must be something good about one who, living in such a room as this and with such a husband as Aylott St. John Aylott, could yet recognize any good in her.

" What do you do with yourself cousin Isola, all day—this kind of thing?" she said abruptly, pointing in disdain to the embroidery-frame where the beadwork pomegranate was still in progress.

" This or something like it," answered Isola a little wearily.

" And nothing more serious? nothing more earnest and useful?"

The young wife shook her head with a painful smile.

" Tell me how you pass your days," said Jane; " tell me just what you do as the rule—we will not mind the exceptions."

Isola told her without parade or exaggeration. She made but a poor show for herself, she knew, but she told the truth, just as things were.

"And this you call life!" cried Jane with an impatient snort; "I call it death! a sleepy, slothful, sinful waste of time and energy, for which you ought to blush, you and your husband too. I wonder at you, Isola! You look good, and you are not a fool I should say—how can you consent to such a life? you, with all your money too!"

"What can I do?" said Isola with a kind of despair in her voice.

"Do? are there no poor to help? no charities to see to? Have you no duties, do you think? Was it ever meant that you should lead a life of nothing but lazy self-indulgence while there is all this misery and wretchedness in the world to try to cure? You are wrong, Isola! shamefully wrong! and so I tell you to your face."

Jane spoke warmly. She felt that she had her word of truth to say, and she said it. Nothing ever daunted her when she was once roused as she was roused now; and nothing silenced. Had she been a guest of the Queen herself, she would have taken her stand on the equal rights of humanity and the almighty power of truth, and would have measured forces as fencers measure foils.

" You forget that my husband would not like me to be active," said Isola in a low voice.

" What does that signify?" snapped Jane. " What does it matter what he likes or dislikes? The question is of absolute right, not of a man's temper. Are you to kill your soul because he likes to kill his? I hate all this slavishness in women!—it is abominable!"

" My dear Jane, what is the good of your being so violent?" remonstrated Mrs. Osborn; " cannot you state your opinion without using such very strong language? You know my great objection to all this unladylike violence."

" It is good for her to have the truth broadly stated," said Jane. " Women like her never hear it—how should they?"

" But is it your place, my dear, to say disagreeable things, true or not? and I am sure in this case quite untrue!" said Mrs. Osborn. " What can you know of your dear cousin's life, which we can all see for ourselves is a most charming one—whether it is according to your own ideas or not? And besides, my dear, what are your ideas? No better than mine or any other person's. If your cousin likes one thing and you like another, why should not her thing be as good as yours?"

Mrs. Osborn said this quite triumphantly. It was not often that she got to anything so like demonstration as this.

"It is my place to tell Isola of her faults!" cried Jane a little excitedly. "It is the place of every truth-loving person to rebuke the sins of others. If I tell her that she is idle and doing no good with her life—that she is pitiful and weak in suffering herself to be made into a slave —and that she owes a higher duty to God and to her own soul than to that mere man her husband—if I try to make her into one of the nobler kind of women with self-reliance and independence, I am only doing my true human duty, and no one shall stop me. I am telling her what it is right she should know. She can do as she likes afterwards, but my conscience at the least is clear. I have shaken my soul free of the sin of countenancing what I hold to be her moral debasement: I have no part in her ruin!"

She said this with a certain religious fervour that made her plain face almost beautiful, if stern still, and severe.

"But what can I do, Jane?" returned Isola. "For myself I should be only too grateful to be of some use in the world. I should like to visit the poor, and go to the Sunday-schools and hospitals. I would not mind what I did that had any good purpose in it; but how can I, when so distinctly against my husband's wishes? He would never tolerate anything like this, and I must please him first of all things."

"By no means," Jane said authoritatively. "Please him first of all things?—stuff! Just because he is a man and you are a woman? What a hideous doctrine!"

"No, not because of that, but because sacrifice is higher than self-will," interposed Isola.

"Sacrifice! rubbish!" sniffed Jane, tossing back her head. "To give up real good for the mere whims of another is no sacrifice righteously put, but a self-degradation—an immoral lying down to Juggernaut. Sacrifice yourself for a good cause if you like—for the progress of principles, for truth, freedom, humanity—but not to foolish whims and fancies like your husband's."

"Good gracious, Jane, where ever did you get such radical opinions?" cried Mrs. Osborn; "I am sure not from me; and if your poor dear father who is dead and gone, could rise out of his grave and hear you holding forth like this, I am sure he would be sorry that he ever made you such a dreadful radical with his free opinions said out as bold as anything before you."

"St. John is not very strong," began Isola.

"Pshaw!" said Jane, "if there is one thing more revolting to me than another, it is to hear silly women excuse the selfishness of men by saying they are not strong. If they are not strong they ought to be, and the sooner they are swept off the face of the earth the better. We don't want weaklings of either sex; and the world would go far better if all the muffs and fools were cleared

off like so many weeds or vermin. But silly people only think of the individual, and not of society
at large; and depend upon it, Isola, we shall
never come to any good till the individual is lost
sight of, and the good of the race alone considered. You may take it as a divine truth—not
acted on yet, unhappily—we are not our own, but
our generation's; and if we can do no good to
that, we had better be done with and put away
the quickest possible."

"Then I hope that I shall never live to see
that day," cried Mrs. Osborn indignantly. "I
am not very strong myself; and if all those who
have weak hearts and poor foolish heads like
mine are to be put to death, I am sure it will
not be a very comfortable or Christian-like arrangement."

"You," continued Jane, turning to Isola and
not noticing her mother's remark, "you are just
as bad as any of them. You think of the annoyance you would give at home if you went counter
to your husband's fancies; you never think of
the good you would do to others—the good that

a strong example does to feeble folk wanting a
precedent for any effort involving pain."

" Well, tell me what I ought to do," said Isola.

" Be free, woman! be yourself; live your own
life, and do not give in to your husband simply
because he is your husband; do not be wicked
because he is weak," said Jane in a deep voice.

" Ah, cousin Jane, it is so easy to say this, but
it is so difficult to act it when you are married!"
said Isola. " And remember this, that sometimes
the life which looks the poorest, is in reality a life
of principle and not of lazy-inclination." She said
this very tenderly, with a moved voice and a lip
that slightly quivered as she spoke.

" Then if you are not selfish, but acting on
wrong principles, you ought to have them shaken
out of you," cried Jane. " I want you to be
more independent than it seems you are, and to
think and act more for yourself than you do."

" A married woman cannot be independent if
she would keep peace, Jane."

" Then have war," retorted Jane. " It is only
one form of martyrdom at the worst; and you

might as well go through that as through the fire and faggot form."

Isola shook her head. It was painful to her to have the formless thoughts just stirring in her own heart placed before her in such naked exaggeration. There was a truth in what her cousin said, and yet a falsehood; and at the moment she was unable to separate the two. She did not understand that what Jane wanted was the informing power of Love; that, iconoclast as she was, breaking false idols and letting the light into dark dungeons—which in itself is a good work—he was not able to build up a temple or to fashion out a creed sufficient for any human soul that lives.

"You say, what are you to do? Well then, I will tell you something that you can do, and that you ought to do," said Jane after a pause. "You know mamma and I let lodgings?"

"Jane, my dear!" cried Mrs. Osborn querulously. "Our house is too large for us, and we give up a room or two," she explained to Isola apologetically.

"We are very poor, papa left us in debt, the rent is high, and we cannot get rid of the house because we cannot afford to put it into repair, so we let lodgings as an income," said Jane decidedly. "And a little while ago we let the second floor back to a young widow just returned from America—a lady, mind! and I know you care for that, and your husband, I should say, cares more. Well! a lady who has lost her husband, children, friends, fortune—everything. She is going to have another child; and there she is, poor soul, without a penny in the world. She had her pocket picked the other day, and she dare not ask her lawyer for another remittance. She is as poor as anything can be that is not an absolute beggar, and we know that she has not enough to eat. Now you know what to do: give this poor soul only a little of your superfluity—show her some human kindness—come to see her; she is respectable—your own solicitor, Mr. Norton, says she is; he knows her and was her reference, so you will not stain your hands by touching hers. Help a suffering fellow-creature,

in all probability quite as good as yourself, and
more unfortunate; and do not ask again what
you can do until you have done this piece of duty
set before you. I am not a very good beggar by
nature, but I *can* beg for this poor tender thing
from one who has such abundance as you have."

Jane's face was grand as she said this : it was
almost the face of an apostle pleading for charity
to the saints in trouble of some beautiful pagan
in power. As was it not, simply differencing the
creed?

" I will help your poor lodger," said Isola earnestly, " and thank you, Jane, for telling me of
her. I have no money of my own"—here she
stopped suddenly, feeling the awkwardness of
the confession—" but I am sure that St. John
will give me some," she exclaimed in an altered
voice; a voice from which the ring had gone,
like the colour out of a flower.

" You have no money of your own, Isola?
Why, who had your poor mamma's portion
then ? " cried Mrs. Osborn all amazed.

" There were no settlements," said Isola, "and
my husband keeps the purse."

Jane shrugged her square-cut shoulders. "And what age are you?" she asked.

"Two-and-twenty," answered Isola.

"Two-and-twenty! well!" was Jane's emphatic rejoinder.

"But I am sure he will give me some for her— I will ask him. Oh yes, I am sure he will!" repeated Isola.

"And I am not," said Jane, rubbing her nose.

"He is very good!" said Isola earnestly. "You do not know how good he is, Jane!"

"No, I don't," said Jane drily. "Good!" she said afterwards, "you might as well call a barber's dummy good!"

"And if he won't give you anything for her, Isola?" asked the iconoclast after a pause.

"Oh! he will!" the young wife repeated, but with a certain falter and tremor of her voice which Jane was sharp enough to catch.

"Humph!" she said a little disdainfully: "it's my belief, Isola, you don't know much about that lord and master of yours, beyond the fact that he *is* your lord and master, and that you dare not call your soul your own if he chooses to say it is his."

"Yes, that is just what I do dare to call my own !" said Isola innocently. "I am not in that state of thraldom, I can assure you, Jane !" ·

"Well then," said Jane, turning straight upon her and fronting her with a very determined face, "if you speak the truth, and do call your soul your own, you must surely consider the right of action as your own, else you have no logical faculty, and are just a goose like your neighbours. And if the right of action is your own, is it not then your duty to do as is best—say in such a case as this—independent of your husband altogether? Do you think it will be any excuse for you when you are weighed in the balance and found wanting, to whine out, ' Please, O Lord, my husband wouldn't let me' ?"

"Jane ! my dear ! O good gracious, did I ever hear anything so profane !" cried Mrs. Osborn in extreme distress. " Why you are worse than your poor dear father, with all his horrid talk of materialism and no hereafter ! Oh dear, what will your cousin think of you !"

"I dcn't care what she thinks of me, mamma, so long as she hears the truth," said Jane sturdily. " So mind, Isola, I hold you to your promise to do this act of charity—come what may."

"Very well," said Isola earnestly, " I do promise. I will help your poor little friend."

" Even if your husband will not ?"

Carried away by the excitement of the moment Isola replied, " Even if my husband will not."

And Jane took credit to herself as she thought, " The first link snapped of the chain round this soul in bondage !—the first breath of fresh air let into this stifling life of arbitrary rule and blind submission—of the tyrannous domination of will, and the slipshod subserviency of good-nature. It is a leverage—and will work through all the rest in them !"

As in the previous visit, Mrs. Osborn continued staying on until luncheon was announced, when a very little pressing on the part of Isola induced her to remain, in spite of Jane's emphatic " No, Isola," and " Come away, mamma, Mr. Aylott will be coming home," and " Mamma,

I cannot stay, I have my work for the ' Comet ' to do." It was of no use. Mrs. Osborn was sub-servient to Jane in most things, but when it came to the wearing of the familiar purple she was immoveable. The usages and an opportunity for indulging in them were Mrs. Osborn's strong-holds, and she had never been beleaguered out of them yet.

So they stayed to luncheon, and Jane revenged herself in her own way by the most disdainful con-demnation of everything she saw. Isola's bedroom she declared to be positively sinful and improper, as well as stifling and detestable. All the orna-ments and semi-boudoir finery about it revolted her; the large cheval glass was an abomination; the toilet-table like a bazaar-stall; what did she want with pen and ink and a writing-table up here? Who but a maniac would sit and write in a bed-room when there were proper living rooms fur-nished and ready? She would bet anything Isola liked there was not a pen that would write, or else there was not one that had ever been written with, and that the ink had all dried away to black glaze.

And so it proved when she went to look; which delighted her grimly enough. At table she positively refused all special delicacies, and took a savage pleasure in being as cynically simple in her tastes as was possible. She would have only plain bread and meat, she said, and asked for beer, repudiating wine disdainfully; she sniffed and said No, "like a bear," said the butler, when he asked her to have this or that with deferential politeness; and made Isola feel as if it was positively sinful to drink madeira out of thin-stemmed glasses bell-shaped and highly polished, and as if sweetbread eaten with a silver fork was the most immoral thing in life, next to ratafia biscuits in a silver cake-basket. She had that way with her when she chose to be unpleasant; was she not an iconoclast whose mission was to destroy other men's gods?

Even when luncheon was over, Mrs. Osborn still stayed entranced; even when the carriage came to the door she stayed, usages or none; it was like tearing a limpet from its native rock to force the poor soul away from this congenial atmosphere, and she clung to the wealth and luxury about with all her strength. At last however it came that they must go, though St. John had not yet returned; and, yielding to Jane's repeated commands, the little woman prepared to leave this pleasant haven and put back into the rougher sea of her daily life once more.

As they stood in the hall saying their last adieus St. John came in, meeting Jane face to face as he came up the step. He swerved aside when he saw her, as men do swerve when they meet something unpleasant and of which they are not afraid; and merely bowing coldly and without speaking, passed into the library and shut the door against them. His face was pale and the lines about it tightly drawn, and Isola felt a strange sickness at her heart as she looked at him when he passed; for there was in it an expression she had never seen before—a fierceness, a wildness, a savage hatred that appalled her as he brushed by her hastily.

When they had gone she hurried to the library, where she found him pacing through the room,

his head bent gloomily, his attitude one of intense dejection, his expression almost maniacal
in its wild despair.

"Dearest St. John," she said, going up to
him and putting her arms about his neck, "do
not mind so much; it shall not happen again. I
will tell my aunt how much you dislike visitors,
and you shall not be annoyed again."

"I have taken care that it shall not happen
again," said St. John gloomily. "We leave
London next week."

Isola started and gave a little shiver. It
seemed so like banishment to her at this moment, excited as she was by all that Jane had
said, and troubled by the mingled truth and
falsehood of her words.

"That is sudden!" she said a little plaintively.

"I am hounded away, Isola. I am hunted
from my home," he said excitedly, again pacing
the room with those restless feverish steps of his.
"You are being taken from me, but I will make
one last effort to keep you. They shall not take
you, Isola, while I have the power to defend you."

He seized her arms as he spoke, and drew her near to him wildly.

"No one shall take me," she said soothingly. "Could any one divide us?"

"I thought not once. I would not have believed that anything could have come in between us. How little I thought it would have come so soon and so easily! Not a week old—an acquaintance of a day—and all our love and our home and my happiness and pride in you gone —gone for ever!" He hid his face in his hands, and Isola saw tears glisten through his fingers.

"Nothing has come between us, and nothing shall," she said, folding her arms round him—a strange feeling of protection towards him as something weaker and less stable than herself for the first time possessing her.

"Ah! you do not care for me now," he said, looking up into her face mournfully. "Our home is broken up—my happiness is gone; I have lost my Isola!"

"It will all come right again when we leave London," she said. "Where have you decided to go?" she then asked, trying to turn his thoughts away.

"Where? I would rather keep it a secret," St. John answered with a suspicious look. "I do not want intruders, Isola."

"And you shall not have them," she returned cheerfully.

But she stifled a sigh while she spoke, bending her neck to her chains again, and shutting out the brief sunshine that had broken through her dull twilight. But she could not shut out the perception that her husband was weak and morbid, and that his feeling for her was not so much love for her or care for her good, as his own pleasure in loving. And the one great golden jewel which all women seek—and how few find! is a man's unselfish love, and the chivalrous consideration of their good before his own pleasure.

CHAPTER VI.

THE INVALID LODGER.

IF Isola forgot cousin Jane's prayer and her own promise while soothing her husband's strange despair, she remembered both as soon as the pressure was gone; but thinking it best to keep silent for the moment and until he was calmer, she said nothing now about the Osborns or money, intending to wait for the next morning, when she would tell St. John the story of the unhappy lady's distress, ask him to give her some money, and further ask his permission to drive to Seymour Street for the purpose of telling aunt Juliana that they were going out of town, and that he disliked visitors when they were in it.

But in her silence her imagination dwelt on the lady's need, till the pain of knowing that here was distress which she might relieve and which was not relieved, became exaggerated and disproportioned. The ruggedness of actual want thus entering her monotonous and orderly sphere—the near presence of a tragedy, and of such a tragedy!—gave her a new emotion, passionate, deep, and painful; and when the morning came she was feverish and excited, feeling as if every moment's delay was a sin and the cause of irreparable disaster. But unlike herself as she was, St. John said nothing out of course. He was a man whose perceptions had to be guided by his own feeling or condition, else he was blind, and a state of mind in another which had no reference to himself always escaped his observation. He was only conscious of his own annoyance with the late events—and that Isola's face looked grander than usual, for the earnest, moved, and thoughtful look that had come into it was as much a dead secret to him as are colours to the blind or harmonies to the deaf.

After breakfast she went up to him as he seated himself in his special easy chair near the little table by the window, at right angles with the couch where she always sat at her embroidery frame.

"I want you to do me a kindness; will you, St. John?" she began, her voice scarcely so firm as usual.

"I make no blind promises; my compliance will depend on your request," said St. John stiffly, as one keeping the future well in hand. "I do not often deny your requests, I think, Isola."

He meant that of his own accord he often did what he intended should give her pleasure because it give him the same; which was another matter altogether; though it is a confusion of motives not unknown to husbands as a race.

"I want you to give me some money," then said Isola.

"Money! and what can you want with money Isola?" His tone was one of half-contemptuous surprise.

"There is a poor lady at my aunt's," began

Isola, speaking fast. "She is a widow just
come home from America. She has no friends,
no money, and has had a great deal of sorrow.
She has lost all her children, and now her
husband on the voyage home; and she is going
to have a little baby, and has nothing ready,
and no money to get anything with. And oh,
St. John! she is hungry and has not enough to
eat," here Isola's eyes swelled up with tears;
"and I want to do something for her," she
continued. "My cousin Jane told me about
her, and I promised that I would help her."

"I thought you had more judgment and common sense, Isola," said St. John disdainfully.
"What do you know about this person? you
know nothing of your relatives even, and yet
you will take their word about an utter stranger,
and mix yourself up in heaven knows what dis-
reputable association. No, I will not give you
money for anything so vague and unsatisfactory.
If this woman is in need, there are the charities
to go to. I subscribe to them, and the mana-
gers know better what to do than you or I."

"But, St. John, she is a lady," urged Isola, the tears gathering bigger as she spoke.

"Lady! nonsense!" was his reply. "Ladies do not come from America in such a state as this. Even if they have no money themselves, they have friends who look after them and prevent such a disgrace as begging: for a lady to be reduced to beg is a simple impossibility. Depend upon it, Isola, she is nothing but a swindler who has taken in your aunt and cousin —if indeed they are not all in league together— and who now wants to prey upon you."

"She did not beg, it was my cousin who told me of her," said Isola earnestly; "the poor thing herself had nothing to do with it; she did not even know that Jane was going to speak to me about her."

"You must not contradict me, Isola," said St. John with grave displeasure; "I know the world better than you do, and you must not set up your judgment in opposition to mine."

"But granting that she is not a lady, she is a woman—a human being in want," pleaded

Isola. "Think of her absolutely wanting food,
and the little baby coming, and we so rich and
happy! It breaks my heart to think of it!
Dearest St. John, do give me some money for
her! I have never asked you yet for anything—
do give it to me this time—do!"

She flung herself across his breast, her tears
falling fast and heavy. Her imagination pictured
the contrast between herself and this unhappy
creature so vividly that everything else was swept
away in her pity, and she had not enough cool-
ness of perception left to read her husband's face,
or to be sensitive to its expression.

"What a silly little child it is to cry for what
it knows nothing about!" said St. John with a
kind of ironical playfulness, turning up her
face and pinching her under lip; but not lovingly, rather disdainfully, and as if she were a
child he was trying to divert from its naugh-
tiness. Isola took away his hand hurriedly.
His smile of levity and contempt jarred on her,
warm and full of emotion as she was, and she
turned away her head with visible repugnance.

This was enough. It was so new to St. John to be repulsed by Isola that for the first moment he was simply amazed, as at any other totally unnatural exhibition; the next, he was deeply wounded; and then the anger which always tinged his pain broke out, and he put her away, saying in a cold voice, "I have given you my decision, Isola; you shall not mix yourself up in a matter so questionable, so discreditable." Not that it was discreditable in any way, but the word sounded grandly mysterious and threatening, so St. John used it as a weapon. "If this person wants charity, let her, as I said, apply to the proper authorities. I forbid your having anything to do with her. Do you hear? I forbid it, Isola," with stern distinctness.

"I must help her, St. John," said Isola passionately, "I shall never be happy again if I do not do something for this poor creature!"

"Isola!" said St. John Aylott; "perhaps you misunderstood me? I will repeat my words. I forbid you to have anything whatever to do with this woman."

" I cannot help it—I must !" sobbed Isola.

Her husband said no more. With the air of a man who has taken some deperate resolution he left the room; and again Isola heard the street door shut as he went out alone to exhale his anger as best he could, leaving her bitterly distressed at this second estrangement, and yet resolute in what she felt to be her duty.

While sitting there, her bead-work pomegranate scattering its ruby-coloured seeds unregarded to-day, the servant brought her in a letter—an untidy letter, written in a large bold hand on office-ruled paper—evidently the first thing that came to hand, as part of spoiled " copy " was on the other side—and folded irregularly and out of all proportion with the envelope, into which it had been thrust anyhow. This was a letter from Jane—an earnest, almost passionate appeal to Isola for the promised help for this poor little woman of theirs. " She was very ill," said Jane, " and mamma had just found out that she had had no food yesterday. Mamma had gone to Mr. Norton about

her as he was her only friend, but no help could
be too much under present circumstances, so
would Isola send what she could spare, and relieve the present want at all events, for they did
not know what help Mr. Norton would give, or if
any, and they were too poor themselves to take
care of her properly. If they did their utmost
they could not get her what was sufficient for her
in her present state. The baby might be coming
—she did not know—and there was no nurse, no
doctor, no provision made for anything. Mamma
was, as Isola could see, but a very helpless body;
she, Jane, knew nothing of these things; Mrs.
Grant seemed utterly prostrate and without
power to direct in any way; and a life might be
sacrificed, to say nothing of the infant's—which
perhaps would be a mercy—all for want of a
little money. And Isola, with so much! Could
she bear to think of this at her grand dinner to-
day? Would her fine wines and made dishes
and expensive fruits taste any the sweeter for
knowing that a human being was starving within
a mile of her? She could not plead ignorance,

and not knowing where to seek for objects of interest and charity, as so many grandee fine ladies did. Her duty was laid before her plain and clear enough, and it would be her own crime and condemnation if she did not do it." With more of the same kind, passionately worded; ending by an earnest appeal to come and see this poor little woman for herself.

Stirred to her very heart, Isola stood in utter anguish for a moment. What should she do? She had no money, and she dared not borrow of the servants; she had no friends to appeal to—no one who could help her. She looked round the luxuriously furnished room, where a fortune lay in pictures, buhl, and Dresden, but all was her husband's; she had no right, now that the collision of wills had come, to make use of a vase, a flower, an ornament. All was hers by office only, not by individual possession; she was the wife to be well endowed because of her position, not the woman of independent holding. Her own possessions were in the same category; chains, rings, bracelets, all this sparkling super-

fluity was his, lent to her for his pride and pleasure in her adornment; she had no right to deal
with it as her own outside that special use.
What could she do? Once she thought of going
to Mr. Norton, but that would have been too
much like open revolt; and yet she could not let
this poor lady starve while she sat in the midst
of such abundance. Suddenly she remembered
her mother's diamond ring, one of the few valua-
bles really belonging to herself—a ring that had
cost fabulous sums when it was bought, which
had always been looked on in the family as an
"investment," and which she expected now
would realize a small fortune if sold. She had
yet to learn the difference between buying and
selling, poor child! That time would come soon
enough; and meanwhile she believed, as do all
the inexperienced, that the buying price and the
selling would approximate at least slightly. She
did not wait to reflect when once this diamond
ring was remembered, but, running upstairs,
opened her dressing-case and, taking it from its
special place, wrapped it into a small parcel; then

wrote a few hasty words to the effect that St.
John had gone out, therefore she could not send
actual money as she had hoped, but she sent
this diamond ring, which she trusted would fetch
a sufficient sum of money to go on with.   She
could not come to see her aunt and this poor
lady, as she had wished; St. John did not like
her to go to people he did not know—she had
already told them they never visited anywhere
—but she would do for poor Mrs. Grant what
she could, and she trusted that Jane knew she
would do all she could.   Then she sent off the
packet by the commissionaire whom Jane had
hired—and a commissionaire's hire, paid out of
her own pocket, was something for Jane in those
days—and waited until her husband came home;
—as the moments wore away the flush and glow
gradually fading and paling, as the certainty of
his displeasure grew stronger and came nearer.

She had never wilfully vexed him before, and
the outburst sure to follow the first serious offence is an anxious time for a young wife hitherto
in unbroken accord with her husband.   But her

conscience upheld her, for all that she was sorry and in fear; and for such a cause as that in which she had disobeyed, it seemed to her that disobedience was a better thing than submission.

"I thought he was a tyrant and selfish!" were Jane's first words spoken to herself as she read Isola's note and understood it. "Mamma is so weak and silly, she sees into nothing, but I was sure of his character. Isola is far too good for him, that I can see. He is a poor creature, and she is worth a dozen of him. But then mamma is taken with him because he is polished, she says, and looks like an aristocrat. Polished! if that is being polished, give me clownishness with a heart and some kind of breadth!"

Grumbling to herself, as was her way when she was annoyed, she put on her bonnet and went out; turning in at the nearest pawnbroker's as naturally and as little abashed as if pledging goods was an every-day occurrence with her, indeed coming rather more easy than buying. She had a struggle about the ring; but the man standing before her grim pigeon-hole knew her

well, and knew that there must inevitably be a
struggle about everything that she came to pledge.
She had been a customer very frequently, and for
some years now—young as she was; and use had
familiarized and sharpened her. However, this
time she was taken in; not understanding the
value of diamonds as accurately as she did that
of tablecloths and silver spoons; and raising about
one-third of what she would have got had she
known finery as well as she knew necessaries.
She got ten pounds only on what had cost a
hundred; but this was better than nothing; ten
pounds being to Jane a very potent barrier against
starvation. And after this transaction she went
about and got such things as she thought best
for the invalid; all done in less time than many
women would have taken to arrange their hair,
and all done in the prompt, energetic, but by no
means soft or graceful manner peculiar to Jane,
full of human kindness as to intent, but rugged,
hard, and ungainly as to form.

Thus, when she went in to the forlorn creature
lying like a dead thing on her bed, she shut the

door roughly and put down her basket noisily; but she spoke in a cheery tone, and with an accent of honest sympathy that almost sweetened her harsh, rasping voice; telling her that a rich cousin had sent these good things for her, and that she must take some wine and soup this very instant, and then she would look better—less like a corpse and more like a living creature than she did now. She did not pet nor caress her, as many women would have done, but she did all manner of thoughtful little kindnesses; and if for the most part noisily and with a rougher hand than might have been, yet with such a real desire to be of use that even the invalid, weakened as she was by fever and bitter thought and the anguish of the future and the agony of the past, yet even she could not but recognize the kindly heart of this so ungainly nurse, and smiled up her faint acknowledgments of the service so frankly rendered.

Presently Mr. Norton came back with Mrs. Osborn. He had been strangely moved at hearing of Mrs. Grant's great need; and though it was his busy time and every hour was worth un-

counted six-and-eightpences, yet so soon as he
knew who it was that wanted him, he shut up his
writing desk, put on his hat, and came back with
his unprofitable client with all the speed that a
broken-down four-wheeler could put forth. He
was strangely white too as he went, and the
moisture stood on his upper lip in thick beads;
but he was just the same in manner as if nothing
was pressing on him with joy or pain, and Mrs.
Osborn was far too shallow to read signs so obscure as Mr. Richard Norton's.

He went upstairs at once; and without waiting
to be announced walked straight into the invalid's
room, not even knocking at the door.

"What a strange violation of the usages!"
thought Mrs. Osborn, fluttering behind him.

"Why did you not send to me at once, Harriet?" asked the lawyer in a low voice; "I
would have helped you without the need of all
this misery. Child! you know that! Indeed I
have a little money in hand that belongs to you
by right, and had I known of your need I would
have sent to you before."

" Thank you, dear old friend," said Mrs. Grant, lifting up a pair of shy dark eyes timidly, " but you have been so kind to me already, I did not want to trouble you again. It was such a stupid thing of me to do ; but you know how unused I am to your London ways, and the pickpockets are so clever !"

" And my little pussy is such a goose !" said Richard Norton looking at her tenderly. " But now tell me—how much do you want ?—five ? ten ? twenty? what? Remember, what I give you is your own. I am only advancing for you ; it is only a loan—no gift on my part. Do you understand ? What shall it be then ? ten ? what ?" in a rather louder key than before.

" I got ten pounds for her to-day, so she can go on for a little while," said Jane coming forward abruptly. She had heard Richard Norton's question, and considered herself entitled to speak.

" Indeed ! Ten pounds is a good serviceable sum, and who sent it, pray ?" said the lawyer turning to her abruptly.

" My cousin Isola Aylott, St. John Aylott's wife," said honest Jane.

"St. John Aylott!" exclaimed Mrs. Grant, starting up with a scared look and pushing back the long dark hair that hung about her pinched and pallid face. "St. John Aylott, do you say?"

"Steady! steady! calm yourself, pussy!—do not let a mere name excite you," said Mr. Norton in a quiet, meaning voice. "No one who knows anything about you, remember!—and no one that you know anything about." He took her hand between both his own and pressed it while he spoke. "Miss Osborn said Isola Aylott" slowly, distinctly, every syllable falling plumb and firm—"Isola Aylott—St. John Aylott's wife, and St. John Aylott is the son of the late incumbent of Greythorpe—people that you do not know and have never heard about before; so there is nothing in the name to excite you," with another strong and meaning pressure of the wasted hand between her own.

"A good name," said Mrs. Osborn striking in, "a very good name—Aylott—but I can't for the life of me help thinking of eyelet-hole whenever I hear it; surgeon and eyelet-hole; so silly, you know!" laughing.

" I cannot bear it !" murmured Harriet Grant, turning her face inward to the pillow and sobbing bitterly as she spoke. " Help from *him !* oh Mr. Norton, dear Mr. Norton, how can I take it ?"

" Take it ? why like a sensible woman to be sure !" said Richard Norton. " It is a kindness done you on Miss Osborn's account, not on yours. Mrs. Aylott is Miss Osborn's cousin, she is not your cousin—don't you understand ?—she knows nothing about you one way or the other, excepting what Miss Osborn may have told her. So no false pride, Harriet ! Take what comes, bless Providence, and make a good dinner as soon as you can. That is the best advice that I or any friend can give you."

Still Mrs. Grant sobbed—her face turned inward to the pillow ; and then Mr. Norton stooped down and whispered something in her ear.

" We had better go out of the room if you are going to talk secrets together !" said Jane abruptly, sniffing.

That was the way in which she did things.

She meant this only for delicacy and care for them, and it looked like offence-taking and brusque annoyance.

"I beg your pardon, I am sure!" said Mr. Norton apologetically. "It is long since I have seen Mrs. Grant, and I have certain things to tell her not to be told before a third person, but I did not mean to be rude to you. I am very sorry if I offended you."

"I did not say you were rude," said Jane opening her eyes, "I only said I would go out of the room if you wanted to talk secrets. I was not huffy and did not mean to find fault; but I thought that if mamma and I were in the way we had better take ourselves off without further bother."

"You see, Jane, how you get misunderstood with those odd manners of yours!" cried Mrs. Osborn irritably—Richard Norton had pleased her.

"Don't be silly, mamma!" retorted Jane. "It is only you who misunderstand me! Every one else knows what I mean, and takes me as I am."

"I don't know about that, Jane," said her mo-

ther crossly. " Look at Mr. St. John yesterday !
I am sure he did not understand you as you call
it ; though what you mean by understanding you
I don't know, unless it is giving in to all your
vagaries. And you are full of nothing but vagaries, Jane, more shame for you !"

" You had better come downstairs, mamma,
and blow me up there," said Jane quite tranquilly,
suiting the action to the word and going out
of the room—slamming the door roughly behind
her.

" Singular person, that Miss Osborn !" said
Mr. Norton, looking after her curiously. " Very
clever I understand, full of strength and energy
and all that, but extremely odd—don't you think
so, pussy ?" He wanted to make her talk, so
that she should not think of mournful things, as
she was thinking now.

" Yes, but she is so really kind !" said Mrs.
Grant with an effort. " I feel safe with her, I
cannot tell you how or why, but I feel as if she
would never let any harm come to me. Perhaps
it is because she is so strong."

" Perhaps so," said Mrs. Norton drily. " Do you know how she became acquainted with the Aylotts ?" he then asked. " You must learn to hear that name without starting, Harriet ! I felt you quiver like a fluttered bird when I said it just now."

" Can you wonder ?" she said, lifting her eyes. She had glorious eyes, large, dark, rich, tender ; but they were not English eyes—they were the eyes of a Spanish gipsy.

" Perhaps not, my dear, but things which are natural are not therefore wise. It may be natural that you should start at this name, but it is not wise and you must not do it. You must remember that there are other Aylotts in the world beside yours."

" Mine !" she said mournfully.

And then the flood-gates opened, and partly because she was weak and suffering she fell into a fit of weeping that soon passed into hysterics, needing other help than Richard Norton's. So the lawyer had to leave with his intended piece of intelligence still unsaid ; and Mrs. Grant was

still in ignorance that when her child was born
and she was strong again, he meant to set her up
in life, provide her with the means of making a fair
start, and in all probability would not leave her
in the lurch if she was fouled in the running.
Neither did she tell him what she had meant to
tell him, that she had made a friend of one Gilbert
Holmes, her fellow-traveller from California, and
that he had left her his address, and should she
write to him and ask him to come and see her?

Neither omission was very important as
things turned out; but the poor little soul would
have been spared some hours of sleepless
anxiety had she known that her future and the
future of the unborn were a little more assured
than appeared now; and if Richard Norton had
given up the whole thing—secrets, mysteries and
all, to Gilbert, it might have been better for all
parties in the end.

Meanwhile the women got the poor widow
through her hysterical attack with such means
and wisdom as they possessed among them;
but the remedy which had the best effect was a

very hearty outbreak of anger on Jane's part,
when, seeing that all softer means failed she
took to rating the shrieking little creature
soundly, and told her she ought to be ashamed
of herself—she was only acting a part and
showing abominable affectation.

And now Isola had to go through her ordeal.
Just about luncheon time her husband returned
from his gloomy musings in the park, and she
must make her confession of what she had done
in his absence. She had never had to confess
anything to him before, and the sensation was
not a pleasant one. Still, it had to be done, for
silence would have been deception, and Isola could
not have stooped to deceit to save herself from
even a worse fate than her husband's displeasure.

He was very angry when she told him; more
angry than he had ever known him to be, than
she had ever supposed it possible that he could
have been. It was not that he used any violence of word or gesture—he neither stormed
nor raved, nor even raised his voice a note
higher; but his handsome Spanish face grew

convulsed and livid with the painful passion
possessing him; his eyes seemed literally to
flash as he turned them upon Isola while she
spoke ; and when she came nearer to him and put
her hand on his arm, he shrank from her shudder-
ing; and she heard him say between his clenched
teeth, " The snake that I have cherished !"

"I am sorry that I have vexed you so much,
St. John," she said very gently, "I would not
have done it for my own pleasure, you know
that !—I would have given up anything in the
world I most longed for, if you had wished me
to do so—you know that, do you not ?" she repeated; "but this was stronger than I !—I could
not let that poor creature want, St. John. Even
though I knew you would be angry with me for
disobeying you, I could not !"

"At least do not make false pretences, Isola,"
said St. John harshly. "*My* wishes, *my* desires, like my commands, have evidently no influence over you. So long as you do what you
wish to do, you care for nothing else. You are
utterly and entirely selfish—you care only to

please yourself in all things, so why disguise the truth ?"

" I did not think I was selfish," said Isola.

" Then you know it now," answered her husband. " I have long known it."

She was silent. From a child she had always had the greatest horror of bandying words; and if it should ever come to that between her husband and herself she felt that the charm of her life would be gone, and that her marriage would be only a legal covenant with all the sweetness of home destroyed. But her silence irritated St. John, disposed as he was to be irritated by everything; and after looking at her for a moment he gave a short sneering laugh, which poor Isola felt rather harder to bear than the most open rebuke would have been. But she still kept silence : indeed she did not well know what to say, and she was afraid of vexing her husband still more than at present if she touched on any unlucky chord, as might so well be in the mood in which he was.

" Well, Isola," he said after a pause, " are you

not going to speak to me? Am I to be fa-
voured by your moroseness as well as by your indifference to my wishes? What have I done,"
he continued, his voice pitched in a certain sharp
key of pain that went through Isola's heart—
"what have I done that you should treat me
as you have done in this matter? I have lived
for you and you only—ever since I married
you I have not had a thought or a wish in
which you were not associated, of which you
were not the object. Has my love tired you,
Isola? Good God! what is the horrible change
that has come over you? What have I done!
tell me what I have done?"

He flung himself into a chair and buried
his face in his hands, groaning, while Isola,
distressed and terrified, did her best to soothe
him; but with scarcely as much entirety of
tenderness as she used to feel for him, rather
with a mixture of pity and surprise at his weakness, and a dim perception of the selfishness
which was the mainspring of his character.
But though she won him back to something

more like his ordinary self than he was at this moment, yet she could not undo the painful impression which her independent action had made. His anger faded away, but left instead the deepest gloom, the blackest melancholy that could well possess a man. He sat for all that day and evening looking moodily on the ground. He would not talk, he would not read, he would not drive, nor stir from where he sat; but there he remained like a graven statue of sorrow, and Isola tried her loving little arts in vain—something stronger than she held the secret issues of his heart.

This state of mind continued for many days, and it took all Isola's natural strength and cheerfulness to bear up under it. It was not that he was ill-tempered, but that he was so intensely sad. He did not scold nor snarl nor sneer, but he gloomed and sorrowed as if he had lost all the joy of life. He never smiled and rarely spoke, and when he did speak it was in the despairing manner of a man who has buried his love. The only thing that seemed to give him any pleasure

was the preparation for their removal to Newfield, where he had taken a house, about a mile
from the Hall where Mr. Tremouille, the uncle
of Gilbert Holmes, lived with his daughter Marcy.
It seemed as if St. John was minded to remain
there for some long time, for he gave extensive
orders to the workmen, and took down many
favourite lares and penates, but he did not tell
Isola what were his plans. He only said to her
very often, "Now you shall be all mine again—
my Isola and no other person's—unshared in
heart and life as before."

And once or twice he looked at her with an
almost terrifying wildness, and asked her if she
loved him as she used to do? in a voice that had
less in it of love than of fiery passion and despair. Poor St. John! he was one of those unlucky beings whom love makes unlovely unless
all is smooth sailing and unruffled happiness;
he was one of those who think that a man's
love is all a woman can desire, and that no
matter whether it be associated with gloom,
jealousy, discomfort, social distress, or home an-

noyance, it is all the same her tap-root of happiness and content. Had any one told him now that he was making Isola unhappy by his strange waywardness, he would have denied it with vehemence, and have said as conclusive refutation, "But she knows that I love her"—as if there could be no appeal beyond that confession.

CHAPTER VII.

MASSINGER'S RESIDUARY LEGATEE.

MRS. GRANT wrote two letters to-day. One was to Aylott St. John Aylott, the other was to Gilbert Holmes at the Travellers' Club. It was not easy for her to confess even to herself what object she had in writing at least one of these two letters. Why should she write to St. John Aylott? Why should she seek to touch his hand once more before she died—to hear his voice, and see his face, and pass away in his arms forgiven and beloved? As if the deed done once and for ever can be recalled at will! As if the sin or the folly committed can be wiped out from the records, and hearts and lives once sundered can be reunited for the mere desire! She wrote as one standing on the brink of the grave, with whom all artificial distinctions have lost their value, and who sees only the great facts of human love and truth; she wrote with fervour, passion, sorrow; but she might as well have prayed the grave to give up its dead as to have trusted that St. John Aylott's perception of love and truth would overcome his respect for artificial distinctions.

He read the letter, at first with a strange kind of angry fear, and then with a passionate disdain which seemed to conquer all the rest. Tearing it into a thousand pieces he enclosed them in an envelope, writing on the fly in a careful, neat hand, "Harriet Aylott is dead; she has been dead for more than ten years, and the person calling herself Harriet Grant is not known to the gentleman to whom she has addressed herself. Further attempts from that quarter will be answered by the police." This was his reply to that yearning out-pour of grieving love, and it was a reply on which he prided himself as showing decision of character and firmness.

Isola, who knew nothing of this letter, sat for some time after dinner with Gibbon's 'Decline and Fall' in her hand, apparently reading, but in reality wondering why St. John had spoken to her so harshly as he had done all through the day, and why he had said to her with a painful smile, more sneer than smile, "It will be strange, Isola, will it not, if in return for all my love for you, and all that I have done for you, my ruin should come through you?"

But he would give her no explanation of his words, and Isola tried to puzzle out their meaning in vain.

The note to Gilbert Holmes was put into his hands just as he was leaving his club.

"Poor little soul! I will go and see her this afternoon. I may be of use to her; I wonder if Richard Norton could do anything for her," he said half aloud, as he walked along the crowded streets to Lincoln's Inn Fields.

It was natural for Gilbert Holmes to be of help to women, and quite as natural that women should go to him for help, being one of the men

who instinctively inspire them with confidence
and the feeling of protection. He was a remarkably handsome man, though by no means of
the barber's block kind of beauty, nor indeed
of any kind often seen in cities or under an
old system of civilization anywhere; a massively-
built man, standing over six feet in height
and evidently proportionately strong—a tawny
man of the leonine type, with a broad square
brow, round which his hair, of the richest
lion-brown, fell in loose and heavy flocks; his
spade-shaped beard was tawny too; his eyes
were of a dark, clear, liquid hazel; and he was
bronzed and burnt till his skin was very nearly
as dark as his hair. He looked as if he had just
come from a state of life where a man's test of
gentlehood consisted not so much in the purity
of his linen and the grace with which he could
undertake the "usages," as in courage, power,
unselfishness, and honour; he looked as if he
had been where realities and not convention-
alisms were of most account, and where humanity was of more value than social observances.

All his gestures had that broad and vigorous freedom which is the essential characteristic of a man accustomed to rely only on his own strength and not on the protection of law; and his dress was as free as his bearing.

An instinctive freemason in the squareness of his attitudes, there was no sloping outline about him, no looking from under his eyebrows furtively, or head turned sideways in a shy kind of fear to be too clearly seen; but he bore himself openly and frankly, standing always face to face, with head erect and chest broadside, his shoulders set well forward, and his feet brought up together and straight as an Indian's—not turned outward from the ankle according to the hideous art of the dancing-master. His eyes were quick and steady, and his hands were well shaped and capable—roughened and knocked about now as if they had done hard work quite lately. He had in all things the look of a granitic man, braced and clamped into more than ordinary power; and yet he was not hard. He could witness death, and order it, and do it with his own hand if the

need came, without a nerve shaken or the hesitation of a moment, but he could nurse the sick and
tend the dying with the gentleness of a woman.
His years of stern experience in a country where
he had carried his life in his hand, so to speak,
had made him fearless, real, and prompt, while
leaving in him that grave gentleness of one who
knows all the natural tragedies and none of the
conventional meannesses of life. He was born
to work and to suffer, but also to overcome—to
win the love of many and the hatred of some
according to individual capacity, but it was impossible that he should be despised.

This, then, was Gilbert Holmes lately returned
from the wilds of California, the fellow-traveller
of Harriet Grant and Massinger's residuary legatee, now on his way to Richard Norton's office
for the purpose of inquiring into that bequest,
and learning, if he could, the extent of his
legacy.

"I am glad to see you in England again; gad!
how changed!" said Richard Norton as Gilbert
was ushered into his office.

"Yes," said Gilbert, "seventeen years in a climate like that of California leaves its mark pretty plainly. I scarcely expected you would have known me again."

"No more I should if I had met you by chance, but I have been looking out for you for some time now. I knew that you were in England and have been expecting you to turn up."

"How did you know this?" asked Gilbert.

"From a fellow-passenger of yours, Mrs. H. Grant," answered Mr. Norton indifferently.

"Ah, poor little soul! so you know her then? I was going to speak to you about her to-day. She excited a great deal of sympathy among the passengers when she lost her husband; not that he was much of a loss to her anyhow, I should say, for he was an ill-conditioned brute enough; but she was so helpless, so child-like, that every one felt for her. I have just had a note from her, telling me she is very ill and lonely. I told her to write and let me know if at any time she wanted any help."

"Indeed!" said Mr. Norton with a sickly

M 2

smile. "You got to be great friends, then, together? I saw her myself a short time since, and, I hope, relieved her more pressing needs. By the by, do you know anything of her family? who she is? what she was before she married? where she originally came from?"

"Not the least in the world, do you?" said Gilbert Holmes.

"No," answered Mr. Norton. And he spoke quite naturally and distinctly.

"She was very reserved about herself," then said Gilbert. "Her husband boasted a little of her family, said she was a lady—as one could see—that her father had been a clergyman, and that her grandfather had sat in the House of Lords; but whether this was bounce or not, no one knew. He was a vile fellow himself—looked and talked more like a groom than anything else; and if it had not been for the poor little woman I should have said the best thing that could have happened to him was what did happen, and that his death was a gain to every one concerned."

"So I think too," said Richard Norton drily.

Then he shook off the subject, and taking up another thread said briskly, " You have come to me, I suppose, about that will of Massinger's ? He was your uncle, I think ?"

" Yes, my mother's brother. Do you know the acting executor, Harvey Wyndham ? his name is new to me as one of my uncle's friends."

" I know him, but not intimately. He is a clever fellow enough—a pushing fellow who knows his business, and who seems to have as many irons in the fire as there are professions to undertake. He is a bit of an artist, a bit of a medical student, he was once a reporter in the House of Commons, now he is sub-editor of a daily paper; he does a little dabbling in the share-market, coaches parliamentary speakers, makes a book, and backs the winner; in fact, anything seems to come easy to him; a kind of handy man generally, and of omnivorous capacity. I know him by the outside of things. He was appointed by your uncle quite lately, I see, with you and Mr. Tremouille. But Mr. Tremouille refused to act, and you were out of England; so

that is how Harvey Wyndham took the business
in hand. You have not seen him, I suppose?"

"Not yet. I found a letter from him at my
agent's when I landed; but I have had so much
to do with other matters, I have not been able to
look after my legacy yet. I appointed to meet
him here to-day. Being a stranger to me, I
thought it best to see him here with you at
first."

"Quite right," said the lawyer. "You know,
I suppose, that there is some little awkwardness
about a legacy, which I have not seen into yet?"
he said indifferently, taking a slip of paper and
writing on it "To see to H. W.'s legacy," as if
it was a quite unimportant matter that he had
forgotten, and of which he needed reminding.

"What legacy?"

"Five hundred pounds to Honor Wilson or
her heirs," said Richard Norton. "That must
be paid first of all, before we can deal with the
residue. Have you any idea yourself of what the
estate will yield?"

"Not the least," said Gilbert.

"Can make no calculation as to the amount of the residue?"

"No; but it cannot be much. My uncle was a fairly successful man, I fancy, for an artist, but, like his tribe, not a saving one. A thousand or two at the utmost when this legacy is paid, I should say; perhaps not so much; I do not know."

"Did you know this Honor Wilson?" asked Richard Norton.

"I never even heard her name before. Who was she?"

"Massinger's model," said Mr. Norton drily. "She is dead now, and we have to seek out her heirs."

"I supposed something of the kind; but fancy my uncle cherishing a passion like this for thirty years!" said Gilbert. "The will is dated thirty-three years back, when I was a little fellow just turned out to school, and she must have been dead many years now, I should say, else I think we should have known something about her."

"Scarcely. You were but young, you see, when you went abroad."

"Twenty-one," interrupted Gilbert, "and older than my years."

"Just so; but men like your uncle do not willingly confide in their juniors; and he and Mr. Tremouille never pulled well together."

"No, they did not," said Gilbert. "I remember my uncle Massinger took it as a sore offence that my uncle Tremouille should have married so soon after his wife's death; and a nigger as he always called the second wife; which made matters worse."

"The second Mrs. Tremouille was a woman of colour?" asked Mr. Norton, glancing off the main subject.

"Yes, a quadroon; and very lovely. I can remember her well."

"You do not know your cousin Marcy, of course?"

"No! of course not. She is just eighteen, and I have been seventeen years out of England. I remember her as a little thing, more like a squealing monkey than anything else, awfully ugly, and as black as a crow."

"She is awfully handsome now," laughed Mr. Norton, "and an heiress."

"Yes," said Gilbert quietly. "She will be well off I should think. Mr. Tremouille cannot have less than two or three thousand a year, and Marcy is the only child."

"I hope she will meet with a good husband," said Mr. Norton in his most matter-of-fact manner.

"I hope she will," said Gilbert.

"You are going to Newfield to see them, of course?"

"Of course. They are my only relatives now, and I should like to see the old place again. You know we had the Hermitage and they the Hall, and at one time divided Newfield pretty much between us?"

"Who knows? so you may again," said Richard Norton smiling jocularly and rubbing his hands with Hood's invisible soap.

"I do not exactly see how it is to be done,"

laughed Gilbert; "I have not come back much richer than when I went. I had made my way pretty well, but the war ruined me. I invested in southern securities, and of course lost everything I possessed."

"Oh! something will turn up," said Mr. Norton.

"But not the Hermitage!" the other answered.

Lambe Tremouille and Archer Holmes, the uncle and father of Gilbert, had married sisters— the sisters of that Massinger, the artist, who had left Honor Wilson a legacy of five hundred pounds. The two men were great friends at the time and both wealthy, so they agreed to live near each other in the country, and to be true brothers in life as they were in connexion. They therefore bought the two Newfield estates, and lived what is called "jolly lives" with infinite satisfaction to all concerned. As time went on things began to change a little; not between them in any way—they were always affectionate and fraternal together—but in certain matters as necessary as even love. They both lived up to the hilt, but Lambe Tremouille

had the longer blade, and Archer Holmes the
shallower holding. The latter woke one day to
find himself ruined, just at the time when Agnes
Tremouille died, and Lambe's affairs began to be
entangled. But the tempers of the men differed
widely. Lambe Tremouille busied himself at
once to repair his disasters, and for this purpose
went out to Jamaica, where some of his entangle-
ments were to be found; but Archer Holmes
went to the Jews, and in a few years, by natural
consequence, to the dogs. Just as Lambe Tremouille returned with his new wife and all his
assets pulled clean and straight, Archer Holmes
died, hopelessly insolvent; and then, the poor
wife dying too, Gilbert saw himself left at the
age of twenty-one without a shilling he could
call his own. He sold the Hermitage, paid the
creditors, threw up his college career, and with his
outfit and a few pounds in his pocket at the end
of his voyage, started off to California, there to
seek what fortune he might be able to find buried
in the gold-fields. He worked hard and he did
well, but, as he told Richard Norton, he invested

his earnings in southern securities; and when the collapse of the confederacy came, the collapse of his fortunes came with it. He had come over to England now to see if he could not create some mercantile interest here, and when he arrived he found that he was Massinger's residuary legatee; which might perhaps set him up in the world again, and redeem all that he had lost. As yet, though he was in the dark as to the value of his legacy, for nothing could be done, said Richard Norton, until Honor Wilson's heirs were found, and though he was on the track, he said—decidedly on the track—he could not say for certain that he had found the right clue; though he might tell Mr. Holmes this much, that perhaps it had some relation to Mrs. H. Grant.

"Perhaps only—pray be careful of that perhaps," he repeated emphatically. "I am by no means sure, and must look into the whole matter, and obtain proofs before paying the money away."

—"I shall be very glad if it is so," said Gilbert heartily, "she wants it sadly enough, poor crea-

ture! for her husband, vulgar, drunken rowdy!
drank and gambled up to the last moment. He
lost his last penny at cut-throat poker not half an
hour before he 'went under,' and of course left
his widow absolutely penniless. We got up a
subscription for her on board and did what we
could, but she landed in a helpless state enough.
I gave her my card in case she should need assis-
tance, and I am going to see her to-day."

"Indeed," said Mr. Norton drily. He did not
seem to like the idea of Gilbert Holmes and this
repeated expression of interest in little Mrs. Grant.

While he was rubbing his hands softly as a refuge from his annoyance, the office-gong sounded
and Harvey Wyndham's name was brought in.

"Show Mr. Wyndham in," said Mr. Norton;
and Harvey, bright, animated, business-like, with
quick black eyes, a ready smile, and a sounding
laugh, came briskly forward, bristling at all
points with business and the importance of time,
and the absolute necessity of settling everything
out of hand at once, as if his life was a pivot upon
which some great national disc was turning.

The business between the three was not of very long continuance. Harvey had only to hand over to Gilbert the whole active management of his uncle's property, taking a release for all that he had done, which was simply the payment of the funeral expenses and some incontestable bills. As he took no benefit under the will, and as the only two clauses in it were this legacy to Honor Wilson and the residuary legateeship to Gilbert Holmes, he did not care to spend his time in continuing the active executorship, he said with his jaunty air of business pressure; and Gilbert said, " Certainly not," quite quietly, and thanked him for the trouble he had taken.

Then Harvey, turning to Richard Norton, asked carelessly, " Has this Honor Wilson been found yet? "

To which the lawyer made reply in his cold legal voice, " Not yet; but I think I am on the track."

" Strange that she should have passed out of all record so entirely! " said Harvey.

" Yes, it is," said Richard Norton; " very strange."

" The waifs and strays are soon lost in a great city like this," said Gilbert. " The wonder is they are ever found again when once they have begun to drift."

" Unless they have good friends to take them by the hand," said Harvey, with the air of one who was in the habit of taking up waifs and strays from the social slough and placing them upon firm clean pasture land rented at his own cost.   He had that way with him—the way of a man who makes capital out of every incident of his life, and who is always on the look-out for occasions of investment.

While they were standing thus, talking of in-different things—for Mr. Norton was not speci-ally busy to-day, and was, beside, fond of talking —again the office-gong sounded and St. John Aylott's name was brought in.   He had taken a house in the country—the Hermitage, Newfield— and he wanted Richard Norton to tell him some-thing he ought to have known before he had con-cluded the agreement.   But it had pleased him at the moment to act with such unwonted promptness and self-reliance; and if he had burnt his fingers in the process, at least he had had his pleasure out of the flame.

When his name was brought in, and Mr. Norton, crumpling up the clerk's bit of paper in his fingers, said aloud, "St. John Aylott! another odd coincidence"—with a curious glance to both the men—Harvey Wyndham called out cheerily, "The husband of the Beauty? Have him in by all means, Norton! I should like to see him amazingly! My father knew something about his father in times gone by, and I have an odd curiosity to see this St. John."

"Show Mr. Aylott in," said Mr. Norton; and St. John's tall, slight figure passed through the doorway, and mingled with the small group standing on the hearth-rug.

What a strangely opposed group it was!—the meeting of four men as unlike in character as could be found anywhere. Richard Norton, the smooth, bland lawyer of the old Encyclopædist school—a man to whom nothing was sacred and nothing forbidden; pitying men and women for failure and for pain, but, ignoring both affection and conscience, thinking sorrow weak and remorse degrading—a Voltairean, as Voltaireans are seen in the nineteenth century in England; by no means bad-hearted—simply without a conscience. Harvey Wyndham, frothy, floating, ambitious, elastic; making use of all things for his own advancement, but with a more fixed force of principle than had the lawyer, inasmuch as he was a liberal and stood with his party manfully, even when dark days came upon them and good things went elsewhere; a man full of surface geniality, seen in the moist lip and the dancing eye; ever ready to serve another, but always with the rapid calculation of how much it would be worth to him either in pocket or reputation; glad to dispense patronage as the means of power, but with no intention at any time of giving away, even in patronage, what he could make use of for himself. St. John Aylott, the shy, reserved gentleman to whom all men below his own grade were common and unclean; who scarce credited the poor with human affections, and who placed a positive virtue in the conventional observances; pure as a child, fastidious as a woman, but stifling the real heart of him under the artificial trammels of Society; and Gilbert Holmes, practical and strong, brushing away all the paltry little cobwebs of pseudoscience and artificial conventions and intellectual sophistry with that great sledge-hammer of common sense which is worth all the theories ever yet set forth—a man who had learned life experimentally and who had not studied it merely at second hand; whose nature had been mortised and consolidated till all looseness and weakness had been driven out of him; and who stood as square and firm on his own feet as his companions were shifty on the one hand, or needed the shoring up of precedent and extraneous balustrading on the other. Leaving out the exaggeration of vices and crimes, what greater divergence of character could there be between four ordinary Englishmen of middle-class education and traditions?

St. John was much anroyed at being thus entrapped, as it were, into an unknown society; but as there was no help for it now, he had to bear his part with the rest—talking in his reserved and cautious manner, pausing a little before he spoke and speaking with downcast eyes, or looking above his companion's head or on the third button of his waistcoat, and never frankly into his face—a manner strangely contrasted with Harvey's expansive cheerfulness and Gilbert's fearless frankness, and which gave an impression of self-defence and the endeavour to conceal, not exhilarating.

A very few moments were sufficient for Gilbert Holmes. He was too much accustomed to all sorts of men not to be able to gauge a stranger; and this moral timidity and reticence of St. John Aylott did not please him. He turned then to Mr. Norton and spoke to him a little apart; while Harvey, with the well-worn ease of a clubman, fitted himself in to St. John's peculiarities, and soon forced himself into quite an attitude of intimacy with the dean's proud grandson. Much to St. John's annoyance; but an annoyance as

helpless as it was guarded. He could not quite
understand Harvey Wyndham. He did not
know why on earth he should be so overwhelm-
ingly civil to him; why he should offer him
tickets to this thing and to that—good things
not open to the public generally and not to be
had for money, but to which he, as a press-man,
had the *entrée*, with the privilege of taking a
friend or friends. What was his, St. John's,
pleasure to him? Why should he wish to gra-
tify him by giving him tickets for good things?
Such excessive good nature was not in St. John
Aylott's line, and he was sorely troubled, because
perplexed with doubts and secret fears, when
manifested to him from another. He did not
know that all this ploughing the ground for
future friendship was because Harvey Wyndham was poor and St. John Aylott was rich, and
rich friends do sometimes open the mouths of
their purses, and let a little golden shower trickle
down upon the thirsty palms of their needier
brethren. But as yet it was labour in vain. St.
John "fought shy" of Harvey's lures, and de-

clined all his baits seriatim. Even when Harvey asked him to dine with him at his club that day fortnight, when a grand dinner was to be given to the great African traveller Fitzwilliam —one of the Cornish Fitzwilliams, said Harvey, parenthetically—even that St. John declined like the rest; though he said unguardedly, "A Cornish Fitzwilliam? I wonder of what branch ! My mother was a Cornish Fitzwilliam."

" Come to us, and then you can learn all about it.   Perhaps you will be able to knock up a relationship between you," said Harvey.

But St. John answered with his shyest look, retreating a step as he spoke ;—" Thank you, no ; I shall not be in town Thursday fortnight ; I am going into the country."

"Lucky fellow !" said Harvey Wyndham. " I wish I was going into the country too!   London is getting unbearable.   Are you going to the seaside ?

" No," said St. John; "into the country."

" Do you know Devonshire ?" asked Harvey.

" No," said St. John.

"The Lake Country ? or Scotland ?"

" No."

" Wales ?"

" No."

"Ah! you should visit all those places!" said Harvey Wyndham gaily, " and I should be deuced glad to meet you there."

But St. John did not take the hint, and tell where he had decided to go.

Then laughing a little boisterously, and planting his feet a little wider apart than before, as he thrust his hands into his waistband-pockets, Harvey said, "Do you know I was nearly taking the liberty of calling on you the other day?"

"Indeed!" said St. John Aylott surprisedly.

" Yes, I know some connections of yours—the Osborns; indeed Miss Osborn is a literary *protégée* of mine; I may say that I dug her out of her obscurity, and have made her, in fact; and when I heard they were going to see you, I very nearly accompanied them for sake of the old name. For my father knew yours well in times past, and one always has a liking for old names.

Interesting people, the Osborns, are they not?
The elder lady quite a study in her way, and the
younger a creature of consummate force!"

"I scarcely know them," said St. John
haughtily. His face changed in expression as
he spoke, and from the mere shyness and reserve
of the former moments, became dark and angry.
"They are Mrs. Aylott's connections, not mine,"
he added hastily; and Harvey understood the
whole nature of the man who could defend the purity of his own blood at the expense of his wife's.

"Yes, so I understand; but they are really
worth cultivating. The surgeon was a slight
mistake, I fancy," laughing. "I know some
fellows who knew him, and they said he was
rough enough; but what of that? Metropolitan
life is too broad and composite to admit of the
narrow class-pride still upheld as an article of
faith in the country. A person is as he seems to
be in the great centres; and if Jane Osborn
becomes, as I suspect she will, a celebrity, the
surgeon will be burked; or rather no one will
care whether her father was a costermonger or a

bishop. Don't you see what I mean? I have as strong prejudices in favour of blood and breeding as any one—taking the matter scientifically and on the principle of selection; but I care more for brains and character. That is my metropolitan education; and you, as a man of the world, go with me, I am sure."

"Not quite," said St. John uneasily. "I confess I am not much prepossessed in favour of Mrs. Osborn or her daughter; I think the one extremely weak and the other coarse, and I do not care to cultivate their acquaintance."

"Then I might not have found their introduction a very safe passport?" laughed Harvey; his light, easy way of taking things was so different to St. John's guarded and formal manner!

"You might have had one which would have been more certain," he answered with perceptible reserve.

"Richard Norton's, for instance?" said Harvey.

"Who is taking my name in vain?" asked the lawyer.

"Only I. I am saying that your introduction

to Mr. Aylott is a better one than what I was on the point of claiming—the Osborns'," said Harvey quite cheerily, and as if unconscious that any offence could be behind his words—as if Mr. Aylott was not at all the man to wince under the allusion, and as if introductions to him were every day matters, as pleasant as they were common.

Mr. Norton laughed. "I think I should be as good a sponsor for you as any one," he said. "I never yet knew St. John refuse a request of mine. I am a kind of half-father to him, and sometimes exercise the functions of one."

No one knew how much he had exercised those functions, nor how much he was exercising them now, in deciding for himself between right and law, and what he would communicate to St. John of his own affairs, and what he would manipulate for him without his consent or advice, not recognizing the young man's judgment or free will in the matters under his hand.

"So you may," said St. John uneasily; "but one grows out of tutelage at last."

"To your family solicitor?" He shook his
head. "That is a guardianship which always
remains in full force, even if the guardian is
changed."

"Perhaps less to him than to any other, but
even with one's family solicitor one must be
master," said St. John a little haughtily.

And Mr. Norton smiled and said, "Yes, certainly, of course," quite naturally, as if St. John
Aylott was the master of his own concerns, and
understood the secrets underlying his life as
clearly as he, Richard Norton, himself understood them. Which at least smoothed the young
man's ruffled self-love and pressed the film a little
closer over his eyes.

"Well now, St. John, suppose you back me
up in what I have said, and show us that you will
do what I ask," said Mr. Norton in his gravely
jocular manner—a jocularity so grave that it
was exceedingly difficult to discover the lighter
lines. "Suppose you ask us all to dinner, hey?
it will be a nice break in that monotonous life of
yours. You know I am always crying out

against it, as bad for yourself and Mrs. Aylott too. Suppose you break through it for once in your life, and let us see your pictures and your cellar. The dean had the best cellar in London in old times. You have still some of that famous malmsey madeira with the blue label left, have you not ?"

" Yes," answered St. John : " I do not often drink it, and my grandfather laid down a pipe of it when my father came of age."

" Fifty-one years ago ?"

" Yes ; if my father had lived he would have been seventy-two now," said St. John a little more gravely than usual.

" And you are thirty ?" asked Mr. Norton.

" Thirty," answered St. John.

There was a slight pause after this. No one seemed to know what to say, for though Mr. Norton might have some reason for being thus exact in his dates, it was really of very little importance to Harvey Wyndham or to Gilbert Holmes of what precise age St. John Aylott was at this moment, and how old his father was when he died.

"But how about this dinner?" then said Mr. Norton, catching up the ball again.

"I should be very glad I am sure," said St. John with an uneasy smile; "but I am going out of town soon. I have taken a house in the country; and that is why I have called here to-day, Norton," branching off in the quick manner of a man escaping a disagreeable subject. "I have taken a place called the Hermitage, at Newfield, and I want to know what would vitiate the agreement? what discomforts or annoyances?"

"The Hermitage at Newfield! what, in God's name, induced you to do that?" cried Richard Norton.

"Why?" asked St. John, startled.

The lawyer turned to Gilbert Holmes. "I say, Holmes, you know what we were talking of just now—the Hermitage?" he called out.

"Yes," said Gilbert.

"Mr. Aylott has taken it."

"Indeed!" said Gilbert, coming forward with a look of interest; "that was my old home before I left England. We had the estate when I

was a lad; but it was obliged to be sold. My
uncle Tremouille lives there still; I mean at
Newfield. I am going down as soon as I get my
business settled in London."

"I hope you will come while I am there,"
said Harvey quite quietly, as if going to the
Tremouilles of Newfield was almost a daily occurrence.

"Are you going too?" asked Gilbert quickly.

"Yes, in about a week's time," said Harvey
with a pleasant smile.

And St. John's soul fainted within him. He had
gone too far to recede now; and at all events, in
the country he could keep these fellows at a dis-
tance, he thought. But what ill luck was upon
him, what evil fate pursued him, that he should
be thus forced into contact with his kind—he
who asked of all men only the grace of isolation?
Here were two links lately forged—Harvey
Wyndham's knowledge of the Osborns—with that
lodger of theirs, and the letter torn into such
passionate fragments haunting his brain like
some horrid spectre that would not be laid: and

now both Gilbert Holmes and Harvey were associated with the very place taken to secure him
against intrusion ! It was a strangely sharp whip
that fate was laying on him at this moment, he
thought; and the expression that passed over his
face was one literally of despair. But no one
seemed to see it, or if to see it, then not to read,
and the general conversation continued—Gilbert
Holmes merely saying by way of rider, " I hope
we shall see you at the Hall, Mr. Aylott; my
uncle is a capital fellow and has first-rate covers."

But St. John did not speak; he simply bowed
in a kind of cold acknowledgment of what had
been said, then turned again to Richard Norton,
and spoke in an under tone as if of some important business affair.

Soon after this Gilbert Holmes and Harvey
Wyndham took their leave together, and as they
walked, the conversation went back to Newfield
and the Hall, and the Tremouilles inhabiting.

" Do you know the daughter ?" asked Gilbert;
" my cousin Marcy ?"

" No; I hear though that she is very beautiful,

and an heiress into the bargain," said Harvey
lightly. " Do you know her ?

" Not at all. I have been away too long. She
was a mere infant when I left."

" I am anxious to see her," said Harvey indifferently. "I have an immense admiration for
these creole creatures. I suppose she is right-
fully a quadroon, but we call quadroons creoles
in general; I mean we call all the mixed race
creoles. I admire all that tropical warmth and
affluence so immensely !"

" Do you ? I like fair girls best," said Gilbert.

" Then we are both out of the usual course,
which gives contrasts as the safer law," laughed
Harvey. " I should take the blonde and you the
brunette. By the by, talking of women, what
an odd thing this is in poor Massinger's will—
this legacy to Honor Wilson ?"

" Yes ; odd, because so long ago. But he was
just the man to stick to an affection all his life,"
said Gilbert. " A secret, a sorrow, and a love—
that was quite his style, poor old fellow !"

" It will be difficult to find the heirs, I should

say," Harvey answered; "they must be adver-
tised for."

"Norton seems to have some idea of who they
are," said Gilbert. "He is a clever fellow and
a cool head. I shall leave the matter to him."

"Can't do better," said Harvey. "Where are
you going to now?" he asked suddenly.

"To sixty, Seymour Street," Gilbert answered.

"No? are you though? That is just where I
am going. The Osborns that I was talking of
live there. Do you know Jane Osborn?"

"No; I am going to see a Mrs. Grant, a little
fellow-passenger of mine."

"By Jove, how odd!" cried Harvey.

"What is odd?" asked the other.

"Oh, the whole thing—Aylott's connections,
your friends, my *protégée*—such a queer jumble
of relations altogether."

"I know things more queer than this," laughed
Gilbert, his hand on the knocker of Mrs. Osborn's
door.

Perhaps something quite as odd in another
way was the cleverness with which Harvey

Wyndham had manipulated all this day's circumstances, and was now manipulating Jane Osborn's
power of work and gratitude: his interview ending with his own reluctant concession to Jane's
blunt and earnest prayer that he would let her
do his work for him while he was away, out of
pure affection and gratitude. She could not, of
course, do his night-work at the office; but there
was much that she could undertake; and did;
Smith of the 'Comet' having no prejudice on the
score of petticoats, and being not in the least dis-
inclined to employ female labour, young or old, if
he could save five shillings a week by doing so—
and Jane no more caring for the rudeness of the
people, the dirtiness of the place, or the anoma-
lousness of her position, than she cared for the
shouldering of the passers by, or the mud upon
the Fleet Street pavement. It caused no kind of
discomfort to her that she was called by the of-
fice-boys Jack Osborn, and sometimes Johnnie
O. for a difference; her work in life, she wisely
thought, was newspaper writing done to time
and up to the mark, and offence-taking at low

impertinence was a folly for which she was far
too wise and strong.

So Jane Osborn was installed Harvey's vice in
his absence : and she would sooner have had this
work to do for him, gratuitous and hard as it
was, than the easiest and best-paid post to be
found on the London press anywhere. Wyndham
had been the first friend she had, and she was
proud to be of use to him—oh, prouder than if
she had been made a duchess!

" You are a first-rate fellow, Jane," said Harvey, shaking her hand vigorously; "I never
knew a woman like you before."

" You need not praise me, Wyndham," she
answered; " where should I have been if it had
not been for you, I should like to know? You
have made me."

" Nonsense, you have made yourself, Jane," he
answered, but with the accent of one who dis-
claims a true acknowledgment from motives of
delicacy and abounding generosity; "I did not
give you your brains."

" No, but you put me where I could use them,"
said Jane.

" And Smith ?"

" Oh, Smith is a good fellow enough," she answered, " but Smith ain't you, Wyndham," her
great grey eyes looking moist and full of feeling
as she spoke.

" Don't look like that, Jane; you look positively handsome," cried Harvey putting his hand
over her eyes.

" Well, of all men living I shouldn't have expected *you* to have been a fool, Wyndham," was
Jane's grave rejoinder.

" I wonder who was the fool between us !"
laughed Harvey to himself when he thought of
that little episode afterwards; adding, " But, by
George, the girl has eyes that would make another woman's fortune."

CHAPTER VIII.

AT THE HERMITAGE.

At the Hermitage, St. John was like a man escaped from a great danger breathing freely again.
The absolute seclusion of the place—for as yet they
had seen no one—restored his feeling of security
in isolation; and as the outward ruling of his
life was what it had always been—monotonous,
orderly, and stately—he had nothing to regret,
having lost nothing that he valued. The 'Times'
came at one o'clock instead of at nine, and there
were green trees to look at and green lanes to
drive through in the place of houses and streets—
else it was all very much the same as in Hyde
Park Square. Isola was as gracefully dressed and

as uselessly employed; he himself was as much as ever the precise gentleman with whom conventional observances ranked before moral virtues; and their domestic arrangements were as formal and luxurious as before—dress, appointments, service, all being as rigidly exacted as if a crowd of gentry and nobles were entertained daily at their table. Wherefore he was happy in thus retaining the cherished circumstances of his town life, while withdrawing his wife from further intercourse with her objectionable kindred, and securing himself from their degrading contact.

In his manners to Isola there was truly a certain subtle difference of tone, which kept up the remembrance of his displeasure—a certain coldness and formality, as if he had been seriously aggrieved and was not quite sure that he had forgiven. He often hinted regretfully at the painful fact of having been driven from his home, and how, through Isola, had come upon him the greatest humiliation of his life. But she never answered him when he spoke thus, and let him sting her with fretful words without retaliation.

To herself this country life of theirs was like the return of spring and childhood. The wild flowers in the hedges, the gleam of golden sunshine across the lawn, the song of the birds in the winding shrubbery to the side, the flies and butterflies, the wooded landscape, the very villages and cottage children had a charm for her which only those know who have been brought up in the country, and who return to it again after years passed in a town. It was in truth a return home. And yet she could not forget the words of that rugged, truthful, unlovely cousin of hers. They seemed to have burnt themselves into her, and to be continually reminding her that she was cowardly in thus consenting to a life which rendered her useless to her kind, giving up the best inheritance of humanity—freedom, and its noblest duty—charity, merely that a conventional law might run smoothly; reminding her too that this sacrifice of every other principle to domestic peace was as base as it was useless. There is no true peace where the conscience is doubtful and the step faltering; and Isola could not conceal it

from herself that her conscience was very doubtful and her step very faltering. Let her give up
every personal inclination, every pleasure natural
to her age, every expression of girlish enthusiasm
both by word and deed, to chime in with her
husband's temper and to make herself more harmonious with his mood; all this was sacrifice,
rightly so-called; but ought she to sacrifice principles that she might meet him at the boundaries
of his own shortcomings? because he was proud
and indolent, ought she to be so likewise? because
he placed his salvation in purple and fine linen,
ought she to forget that hers lay in truth to
human nature and charity to her fellow-creatures?
did the righteousness of wifely submission include unrighteousness to the light within her
own soul?

Day by day these thoughts grew in her, till at
last she resolved to act on them; and, fulfilling the
duty that was nearest to her, determined to risk
another scene of discord, and ask her husband
for money of her own to keep or spend as she
chose, and for permission to visit the poor and

learn their lives and their wants. But she did not
do this just yet. She knew her husband too well
to risk refusal by over-haste. How often had she
not had to learn that lesson of patient waiting!

The village of Newfield was one of those beautiful English villages nested among trees, which
are like lovely sleepy hollows set in a corner
apart—a place where the rich pastures are filled
with herds of cows standing knee-deep in flowery
grass under bordering lines of woodland or clumps
of stately trees—where the bright stream, running
through the copse, broadens out into a wide pool
for the mill, and where the mill-dam is the local
Niagara to the village children, filling them with
childish awe at the great forces of nature—where
the cottages are. all clothed in climbing plants,
and the old grey church is overrun with ivy—
where the smithy is the centre of news, and the
farmer, riding to cover, is as grand a man as the
parson or the doctor—where railroads and great
trunk roads, canals and large towns, and all the
rest of the carrying power and centralizing force
of England are almost unknown—where life is

sauntered through in a lazy lotus-eating way that sets all things half asleep—and where the world's tumult and its anguish seem to have been passed by as not pertaining to the humanity sheltered there.

It was the very place for St. John Aylott; where he was reverenced and isolated at the same time, looked up to and let alone—as was his ideal of a gentleman's existence ; and he wondered that he had not thought before of living in the country, where he could be the local Dalai Lama at no cost to himself beyond his permission to be worshipped. He grew quite animated in planning out his future at Newfield; and Isola encouraged the idea, thinking that they should both lead freer, and by so much better, lives in the country than they did in their luxurious isolation in town. So for the next few days there was an active correspondence with Richard Norton and the agent for the owner of the Hermitage ; and the activity did St. John good, and made him feel quite a man of business and of large social importance.

But he would not give Isola an independent allowance, for all his serener humour. He was not angry when she asked him—which was something gained—but he put her off with half-jeering yet not unkindly refusals, and at last said very plainly, No, he was the master and the person to apply to in times of need. He would not share his duties, he said grandly, even with a wife. He did not say that he would go into their miserable hovels, nor come into personal contact with the poor anyhow; but he would instruct an agent to report on the most deserving cases, when perhaps he would relieve them.

This was all that Isola could get from him of genial charity for the poor; but it was better than nothing, and she was wise enough to know the full value of that phrase. Meanwhile she ordered soup and gruel in the kitchen for those who chose to ask; but because she was not suffered to look after the execution of her own orders, not much good was done in that way. Either the cook wasted the material, or the kitchenmaid refused the askers, or the footman took a fancy to the broth for his luncheon, or some recondite kitchen catastrophe intervened, and the Hermitage was as yet a well of oil not flowing for the good of the poor of Newfield.

One day St. John and Isola were walking in the lane near the house. St. John had never walked in London; but since he had been in the country he had sometimes undertaken an evening stroll as his recognition of natural conditions, and condescending willingness of adoption, when he thought he could do so without loss of dignity. He had bought riding horses too, and was going to ride about the country with his wife, who as a girl had been capable of anything that would bear a saddle at all. A profound instinct of jealousy had prevented his riding in London. Isola would have been too much seen there; her hat would have been too becoming; her habit would have shown her figure to too great advantage; she would have been followed perhaps—perhaps she would have seen a face that would have smiled on her as she passed, and she might have caught the smile and have returned it, or remembered. He

preferred to such dangerous chances as these his
close, dark-green brougham, where he could sit
in the corner with her by his side, and look out
unseen on the moving panorama.   Here at Newfield it was different.   There was no one to see
her save a few rustics, who ranked as little higher
than the beasts they herded in St. John's mind;
and she might ride where she would in the full
security of loneliness.   She could meet no one
among the lanes and cornfields who could either
claim her, as had those odious relatives of hers,
or who could smile upon her pleasantly, and so
haunt her memory with dreams that might warp
her allegiance from him.   Wherefore he ordered
a couple of showy park hacks through his coach-
man, and was now waiting their arrival; and
meanwhile he walked at times in the cool of the
evening for about a mile or so along the lanes.

They were walking now.   It was a warm June
evening, fragrant, fresh, abounding with the life
of the young summer.   The hedges glowed with
flowers; the birds were twittering in the trees;
here and there a blackbird gave out his rich and

lusty note, and here and there a thrush sang with a sweeter passion; shy evening moths flitted about; swifts and swallows skimmed over the pools and along the river; the western sky was a dappled dome of crumbling gold, and the trees stood all aflame against the light; but just in the east, blotting out the silver thread of the young moon, hung a heavy purple cloud, threatening and ominous, betokening storm in the future if not now in the immediate present. The lane in which the Aylotts were walking was one which led to the Hall if followed to its end—a kind of by-way or occupation road, where two carts could not pass each other, and where to meet a herd of cows was a rather formidable matter to London-bred nerves. It widened out into a broader sweep at a place called Buckhurst Ground, where was a group of three picturesque cottages belonging to Mr. Tremouille of the Hall; but save this small clearing it was just a narrow line between two leafy walls starred with wild roses and draperied with clematis.

As they walked on in the evening loveliness,

Isola in a kind of dreamy heaven, and even St. John quietly content, they came face to face with two gentlemen and a lady, sauntering as slowly and as silently as they between the scented hedgerows. Instantly one of the gentlemen came up to St. John; and, holding out his hand, said in a cordial, hearty manner—quite the manner of an old friend who had the right of familiar greeting—" This is a pleasant chance ! Mr. Tremouille, this is my friend Mr. Aylott, of whom I was speaking only half a minute since. Miss Tremouille, and I presume, Mrs. Aylott ?" interrogatively.

It was all done in a moment—done in Harvey's off-hand, dashing, free-and-easy manner that was not conventionally vulgar because so entirely conversant with the rules, but that had not a shade of moral reserve or refinement in it.

" I am glad to see you," said Mr. Tremouille going up to St. John and offering his hand quite as cordially as Harvey Wyndham had done. " My daughter and I were going to call on you at the Hermitage to introduce ourselves, and this is a fortunate meeting—breaks the ice as one may say. Marcy, my dear !"

Marcy Tremouille came forward with a lazy languid grace, and offered her small hand prettily to Isola.

"I am very glad to see you," she said in a soft flute-like voice, with just the daintiest little dash of foreign intonation in it. "We are all so dull here, that your coming is quite a godsend; you must come and see me very often please, and let us be great friends together."

"Thank you," said Isola smiling; while even St. John looked at the lovely face which had broken into his charmed circle of isolation with admiration and forgiveness, and for sake of it forgave the others.

And in truth it was a lovely face; the face of a Caucasian generously tinged with dark blood, and with all the beauty of form and colour peculiar to the mixture of the north and south. The sleepy almond-shaped eyes were of the deepest and richest brown, and the thick curled lashes gave them a shy and starry look, at once innocent and enticing; the eyebrows were a long wide arch, and as finely pencilled as if they had been painted with a brush; the mouth was somewhat too full perhaps, and there was a certain looseness and mobility about it not quite pleasing, but it was richly coloured and beautifully shaped; the figure was supple, slight, and full of swan-neck curves; the curling hair was dead-black, and broke in rings and ripples over the smooth brow; and the skin was of a low olive-tint, harmonizing perfectly with the depth of the night-black hair and the full carmine of the lips. It was the loveliest thing of the kind to be seen, and would have sent the artists who used to illustrate the 'Books of Beauty' and 'Forget-me-nots' wild with delight at its fitness for that kind of art. But it was beauty only—no more; for though Marcy had a certain kind of intelligence in her face she had no real power of mind, and it was cunning rather than intellect that it expressed. But she was the first woman whom St. John had looked on with pleasure since he married, or whom he would care to see again.

Old Mr. Tremouille too was a pleasant-natured man, one of those good-hearted and morally indolent people who let things go their own way, and have no thought of interfering with any one provided no one interferes with him; a genial, generous, kindly man, with whom hospitality was a principle when people came in his way—though he never sought them out— and to whom therefore any hesitation in accepting what he went out of his way to offer, was an offence: which gave a certain insistance to his manner, that generally overpowered his company and carried his wish, whatever the amount of original reluctance. As now; when St. John Aylott found himself in a manner overborne by Mr. Tremouille's cordiality, and forced to accept him on his own terms whether he liked them or no.

The old man had made up his mind to call on the new comers at the Hermitage, whatever they might be; that was the duty of his position, what he owed to himself as senior grandee of Newfield; but he had not made up his mind to be cordial, nor to undertake anything like in-

timate relations. Now however, when he saw
for himself that St. John was "a man of fashion
and breeding" as he called it, and that Isola
was "one of the loveliest women he had seen
for many a long day," he was resolved that
they should all become very well acquainted
together, and that there should be no nonsense
nor formality between them. So he gave first,
a hearty general invitation which meant everything and nothing, and then he specified to-
morrow for luncheon and looking over the im-
provements.

A country gentleman, heart and soul, he
could not understand how any man should
not have as profound an interest in stables
and pigsties as himself; and when he mentioned his new racks and his patent mangers, he so evidently put forth the weightiest
attraction he possessed, that St. John, with the
quick tact of a gentleman, saw he must not
despise the lure, but must accept it as one both
dainty and potent. Indeed, he was a little
ashamed of himself for his own deficiencies in

that direction, and resolved to become a country gentleman forthwith, and to be interested in pigsties and patent mangers according to his ability.

Marcy too added to the charm of the lure; for when her father spoke about the Aylotts' coming to the Hall, she went up to St. John with the sweetest and most caressing air, saying in a soft coaxing voice, " Oh, do come, Mr. Aylott! Come and see my new lory and all my live things!" as if she had therein offered her weightiest attraction too, and thought it just as impossible that any man should vote lories a bore, and live things generally a nuisance, as Mr. Tremouille thought it impossible that a farm-yard or stock-raising should not be of supremest pleasure and importance.

To all of which St. John consented with a facility and, for him, warmth of manner that almost startled Isola, it was so unlike anything she had ever seen before. But she was too well pleased to criticize very closely. She did not know how much she hungered after a wider human intercourse until it came in her way;

when she could somewhat measure her delight; those two gauges of desire, grief for the lack and joy at the advent, not being necessarily of equal force.

After a little more talk on indifferent subjects, the two parties coalesced—the Aylotts continuing their walk and the Tremouilles turning back with them, and walking as far as they intended to go, the bourne named being Buckhurst Ground. It was a very pleasant walk to every one. St. John and Mr. Tremouille went on in front talking about crops and hunting: or rather Mr. Tremouille talked and St. John listened: while Marcy and Isola, a little way behind, were attended by Harvey, to whom at this moment fortune seemed more generously minded than of late. The evening was delicious—the two women beside him were among the most beautiful of their kind—and if the one was nobler, grander, but also unattainable, the other was beautiful beyond words, and rich, and to be won. So the floating literary handy-man was satisfied and at ease, and talked to his companions cheerily—Isola answering for the most part, while Marcy's soft note struck at intervals through the somewhat metallic ring of Harvey's sounding words and the deeper melody of Isola's voice, like the tinkling of a silver bell.

Presently they came to Buckhurst Ground, where Mr. Tremouille called out to a fair-haired, pretty-looking woman standing before the door of the third cottage in the group, " Well, Nancy, and how's father to-night ?"

" Nicely, sir, thank you," said Nancy dropping a curtsey.

" Cough better ?"

" Yes, sir."

" Doctor been to-day ?"

"Not to-day, sir. Father says he needn't mind to come again, he thinks; he's mending fast, he says."

" Glad of it. Tell him I called to ask after him ; and come up to the Hall to-morrow, Nancy, do you hear? We'll have something, maybe, that will suit his complaint—who knows ?" with a broad and hearty smile.

"Thank you, sir," said Nancy, with another curtsey; and the walking party passed on.

"Who is that?" asked St. John, partly for want of something to say.

"That is Nancy Wilson, old Aaron Wilson's granddaughter," answered Mr. Tremouille, "a thoroughly worthy young woman, and he is a first-rate old fellow. I must tell you his story some day. It is rather painful, but he has borne everything with such uncomplaining resignation, that one cannot help respecting the beauty of character which lies under his rough outside. I am fond of the poor—are you?" to St. John.

"I do not know much of them," St. John answered, "and those I have known have not been very favourable specimens; at least they did not interest me."

"That is a misfortune. If you want to live well in the country you must take an interest in your tenants," said Mr. Tremouille. "No good work is done that has not the master's eye over it continually, and the closer the tie between landlord and tenant, the better the work and the more stable the relations."

"I suppose so," said St. John a little stiffly; "but those low fellows want keeping at a distance too."

"Oh, they always know a real gentleman!" said Mr. Tremouille cheerfully. "It is your half-and-half fellows who are so deuced afraid of their own dignity that the lower orders despise and detect —Lord! as keen as a hound scents a fox! But with the real thing there is no danger. They can unbend as much as they like, and never get taken advantage of. Oh! it is a wonderful solidifier, is that blue blood. There is nothing like it!"

"Nothing," said St. John Aylott emphatically, feeling thankful beyond the measure of most moments of thankfulness that his blood was all blue— pure to the last drop, and that no muddy stream had ever polluted it within the records of history.

"What a good face that woman had—but not an English face either," said Isola as they passed. "Who is she, Miss Tremouille?"

"Nancy Wilson, I believe; tenants of papa's," said Marcy languidly.

"For all that she has fair hair, she has quite a Spanish face in contour," said Harvey.

"Yes, I thought it looked foreign," Isola answered.

"Ah! I see you are a physiognomist, Mrs. Aylott; so am I; a most interesting study, don't you think so?"

"I do not understand it as a study; I only judge instinctively," was her answer.

"As we all do more or less," said Harvey. He was famous for putting people on good terms with themselves. "Are you very rapid in your judgments, Mrs. Aylott? very distinct?"

"Generally, I think. Do not you know at first sight, Miss Tremouille, whether you like or dislike a person?"

"Who? I? oh! I am so stupid," said Marcy with a slight lisp. "I have been listening to you and Mr. Wyndham with such pleasure! I like to hear people talk, but I am such a silly child myself, I cannot. Please go on again! it is so pleasant to hear great clever things like you two talk."

"But I am not a great clever thing at all," said Isola laughing and blushing deeply.

"Oh yes, you are!" said Marcy. "I can see that you are, and I am such a little goose."

"Do you never change your first impressions, Mrs. Aylott?" struck in Harvey, with a peculiar look to Marcy.

"I do not say that," she answered; "first impressions are strong, of course, but instincts are not before reason."

"Many women think they are," said Harvey. "Indeed, how many women ever reason?"

"And I do not think you like it very much when we try to do so," said Isola ingenuously.

"Pray do not include me?" cried Harvey. "I am notorious for my admiration of women with bone and muscle in. them. Ask your cousin Jane Osborn!"

"You know Jane Osborn then?" she said with a brightened face.

He laughed. "I should think so! Know Jane Osborn? why she is my literary child—my creation—my discovery—my bit of brute matter on

which I have carved one word—success. Know
Jane Osborn! why I dug her out and brought
her into notice. Yes, I know her very well, I
am glad to say, and respect her immensely! A
splendid creature intellectually—so strong and
square and capable! She is a first-rate woman!"

"I am glad you like her so much," said Isola
warmly.

"Which means that you like her?"

"Yes, very much indeed."

"Then that was a friendship at first sight?"
Harvey said with a certain indefinite meaning
in his voice.

"Quite," answered Isola innocently.

"And I do not think you will ever have cause
to change," said Harvey. "I think I have
gauged my friend Jane completely, and I am
sure that she is what the Americans call real
grit from head to heel."

"I am so glad!" repeated Isola. "I am sure
she is good! I never heard any one whose
words made such an impression upon me as

hers—never knew any one whose whole nature seemed so clear, so bright, so pure!"

She said this enthusiastically; and then she blushed deeply. She, who was so little used to tell her thoughts even in the most halting fashion, to be now speaking to this stranger as confidently as if she had known him for years, and speaking with such warmth of a woman for whom her husband had taken such a deep dislike! And her blush, and the girlish trouble of conscience that came into her face veiling the stronger womanliness, made her more beautiful than before to Harvey, and set him speculating as to the real nature of St. John Aylott's wife, as he was not much given to speculate about the nature of women. For Harvey, like many men of large professions, had in his heart a very profound contempt for women, excepting as beautiful creatures sent into the world for the pleasure and advantage of men—their relations to men the final cause of their being. He had all the talk and manner of one who valued them on higher grounds; but the talk was froth, and

the manner surface, and the half contemptuous
and wholly selfish love was the only reality.

"I am very glad you have left London and
come to Newfield," he then said suddenly.

"So am I," answered Isola, looking at Marcy
with a smile.

"Yes, it is so nice of you to make such good
friends with us all at once," said Marcy. "You
know Mr. Wyndham before, did you not?"

"No! I never met him before to-day," said
Isola.

"Indeed!" said Marcy in a tone of surprise,
arching her eyebrows.

Something in the tone of her voice brought
the blood again into Isola's face, and her blush
was not lessened by Harvey's turning to her and
saying gallantly, "But though we have met only
for the first time, Mrs. Aylott, we understand the
Elective Affinities, do we not, and intend to ex-
emplify the doctrine?"

Before she could speak, with the warmth of
the setting sun still further heightening the glow
on her face, St. John Aylott and Mr. Tremouille

turned round, and St. John caught the blush and the downcast eyes, and the look of pain and embarrassment in Isola's face, as if he had caught the sharp edge of a knife upon his hand.

"We must go home, Isola, if you please," he said in his cold lordly manner.

"I am ready," she answered cheerfully, shaking hands with Marcy, who said, by way of adieu,

"And thank you so much for that nice talk with Mr. Wyndham about Elective Affinities! It was so nice and clever of you to talk as you did!"

"Remember to-morrow—two o'clock punctually! You will not forget?" said Mr. Tremouille, holding Isola's hand while she spoke; and St. John's sensitive jealousy underwent another pang at the fatherly familiarity.

"No," she said smiling. "We will not forget; we will be sure to come, and punctually."

"That's right," said Mr. Tremouille shaking her hand warmly. "That's honest and straightforward, and that's what I like. We are the only neighbours in Newfield besides the vicar's people, who don't count for much, so we must be

good friends, don't you see, and make the best
of each other."

"You are very, very kind," said Isola with a
smile.   "It is so good of you to be so friendly to
us."

"Do you play croquet?" asked Marcy of St.
John.   "I hope you do!   I love croquet, don't
you?   All nice people should play.   I hope you
do."

"Not much," answered St. John.   He had
never handled a mallet, but he never liked to acknowledge his ignorance of anything.   "But I
suppose I can learn in time?"

"I will teach you," said Marcy.   "Papa and I
often play with two balls each; but it is so much
nicer when we have more players — more fun
every way.   Does Mrs. Aylott play?"

"No," said St. John; and he thought of Isola's
pretty feet and her dainty boots, in which he
had always taken such immense interest, and
then of Harvey Wyndham's eyes.

"You will let me teach you both?" she said
in a pretty pleading voice.   "Or I'll take you,

Mr. Aylott, and Mr. Wyndham can teach Mrs. Aylott—shall it be that way?" quite anxiously, as if learning croquet and who were to be the teachers were quite the most important questions of the time.

"Yes, that will be very pleasant," said St. John; and he forgot Isola's pretty feet and Harvey Wyndham's roving glances when Marcy Tremouille looked into his face with her sleepy starry eyes, and said to him caressingly,

"May I not teach you, Mr. Aylott?"

The glow of this new pleasure faded away as soon as he was alone with Isola again; and he was cold and silent for the rest of the evening, because Harvey Wyndham had walked with her through the lane, and they had talked of Elective Affinities together.

He had never yet probed the depth of his jealousy, because he had not had reason to do so; but, in truth, he was almost insanely jealous, and grudged the merest commonplaces of civility to his wife. He wanted her to be dependent upon him only, and felt it as an offence that

others should even see her beauty or admire
it, or that any one but himself should make an
hour of hers pass pleasantly. And yet all that
he did for her was on his own account, not on
hers; he gave her what he wished her to have,
not what she desired; he was generous by the
grace of power, not by the recognition of right;
what he bestowed was a dole and not a due.

The next day they went to the Hall, and after
luncheon they strolled through the grounds.
And St. John was shown all the newest im-
provements, and instructed in some of the pleasures and responsibilities of a country gentleman's condition. And as he thought of settling
for good at the Hermitage, buying the estate and
becoming a country gentleman himself, he took
what was for him quite an animated pleasure
in hearing all about the patent manger, and
the new racks, and the original system of ven-
tilation, and the best form of the loose-box, and
all the rest of the stable arrangements. And as
Marcy was with him and her father, the lesson
was doubly satisfactory. But by this arrange-

ment Harvey and Isola was thrown together alone, and Harvey made good use of the opportunity, and talked as—Harvey Wyndham knew how to talk to women.

His talk was very delightful to Isola. She knew too little of the world to be able to understand the true value of clever froth, and for all her strong sense and the instinctive adjustment of a nature at once large and pure, she could not quite rate Harvey Wyndham as he deserved. So she let herself be moved and fascinated by his half poetic, half metaphysical cant, and thought how delightful it would be if St. John would sometimes talk to her in the same way. Intellectual life of any kind was new to her; and to hear herself analyzed and her thoughts and feelings understood even before utterance, was something too strange and fascinating to leave her judgment very clear. Thirsty lips stoop to brackish water, and on the first draught think them sweet.

"I believe I could make that woman love me!" was Harvey Wyndham's thought when they parted. He saw the ready colour rise in Isola's face while he pressed her hand, not by any means with lover-like secrecy, but in an honest, friendly, hearty manner, and yet as if there was a secret understanding between them somehow. " Gad !" he continued mentally, " if it were not for this little thing here, I would ask no better occupation than that of wakening up this Isola Aylott. Splendid creature she is, and worth all the bother of making love to ! But I must not spoil my chances of a good settlement for the mere sake of a pretty face and a glory of golden hair. Isola Aylott has a husband, worse luck ! and Marcy Tremouille has a fortune ; and though beauty is very charming, the three per cents. are safer !"

CHAPTER IX.

ARE YOU A ROVER, MR. WYNDHAM?

The croquet lesson could not come off on the day of the Aylotts' first visit to the Hall. There had been a heavy storm during the night—had not that ominous purple cloud foretold it?—which rendered the ground unfit for play; so that the initiation into the mysteries of croquéing and roquéing, and the properties of hoop, ball, and mallet had to be deferred: which gave occasion for another invitation to the Hall and an excuse for its acceptance. A day or two after the first visit then, the Tremouilles meanwhile having been to see them at the Hermitage, the young people were once more at the Hall, and Marcy's one active pleasure was soon in full force.

It cost St. John a pang to see Isola "coached" by Harvey; but what could he do? Marcy took possession of him as a matter of course, and Isola's appropriation by Mr. Wyndham followed as a necessary consequence. Yet pleasant as it was to him to be coaxed and flattered by pretty Marcy, and much as he liked her lessons and the innocent manner of coquetry with which she gave them, he was none the better pleased with Isola's instruction, and made her understand that he was annoyed; but at what, neither he nor the peccant wife could have exactly defined.

Isola herself was not quite at ease. There was something about Harvey Wyndham that attracted while it repelled her; a certain mixture of familiarity and admiration, and the flattery of assumed intellectual equality, and the good comradeship of an artist, which was all too strange to her to be thoroughly well liked; but she set down her natural shrinking to her own ignorance of the world, and supposed that this kind of thing was all right and that she was simply prudish and uninstructed. All of which Harvey understood like an open book, and played on, like a master trying the chords of a new organ, to learn the pitch and power of vibration.

" Now Mr. Aylott, come to me !" cried Marcy's silvery voice. " Touch me very gently, put me in position, and then croquet Mrs. Aylott. You must send her away as far as you can—to the very boundaries if you can."

" Oh ! that is very cruel !" laughed Isola.

The personality of the instructions amused her. She was only a married nun remember, and knew less of social life than many a school girl. And this was her first game of croquet.

" It is the game," said Marcy gravely. Croquet was a species of religion to her.

" That is, if I can do as you bid me," said St. John, making his stroke.

" Oh ! you have missed me !" cried Marcy. " Why did you not do as I told you and come to me !"

" I tried, but I could not," said St. John just a shade sulkily. " I am only a beginner you must recollect, and I fear a very stupid one," stiffly.

"No! you are not at all stupid!" she said;
"Papa was much worse than you are when he
began, and would spoon oh! for ever so long!
and never would remember his hoops! But
you should have tried to come to me when I
told you."

"Now then for my pupil!" laughed Harvey;
"take care, Mrs. Aylott, and do not disgrace
me, nor compromise a very good game."

"What am I to do?" she asked.

"Croquet your husband," said Harvey.

"Poor St. John!" she laughed merrily, looking at him with a pretty girlish expression of
playful deprecation as she struck "black,"
his colour.

"Capital!" cried Harvey; "now send him
away very hard, anywhere into space that seems
most convenient to you. Mind you do not slip
your foot! Here! you have not got the balls
right—allow me." He knelt down and pressed
the balls more firmly together, and at the
same time placed Isola's foot in its proper
position. All in the way of business and the

game, and done in the most simple and matter
of fact manner, but St. John blanched with
sudden pain; a pain by no means soothed when
Isola made a clean chance-stroke, and sent his
ball right across the lawn.

"Famous play!" cried Harvey, "first-rate!
Now black, you will have to make up for lost
ground!"

"I am very much obliged to you, Isola,"
cried St. John ironically as he passed his wife.

"It was quite fair!" said Marcy; "I would
go and pick you up but you are so far off,
and I could do no good. Never mind! you
must come to me and I will put you through
your hoop."

But Isola felt that she had displeased her
husband, and began to have a fear of croquet
as a diversion.

"I hope that you are content now you have
ruined me," said St. John to her unpleasantly,
as he gave his ball a weak stroke, and did
not send it a couple of feet onward.

"I am so sorry!" she said tenderly.

"But it was the game!" said Marcy; "and
if you had come to me, Mr. Aylott, when I told
you, it would have been all right; she could
not have hurt us! Now we must do the best
we can to make up for lost ground; but Mr.
Wyndham," shaking her head archly, "you are
such a naughty man! you are such a wicked
enemy to me always!"

"But see what I have to protect!" said
Harvey pointing to Isola's ball that lay in
tempting jeopardy near Marcy's; "a lamb against
a dragon!"

"But you are a dragon too!" said Marcy,
"and a naughty wicked dragon too!"

"Not to Miss Tremouille!" said Harvey in an
under tone; "to her I am—"

"Now go and flirt with your own partner,
Mr. Wyndham!" interrupted Marcy rather
shrilly; "I will not be coaxed over! I am
going to croquet her away, and I will do her
and you all the harm I can, and protect my own
lamb like a heroine; so don't make soft
speeches to me; go and console blue!"

And laughing, and shaking her pretty small head playfully, she went on with the game; but by some unaccountable chance she made a bad stroke, and Isola's ball rested untouched upon the lawn.

"How provoking!" said Marcy pettishly.

"Better luck next time!" sang out Harvey, as he went through a series of brilliant manœuvres that put himself and his partner out of danger.

As the game went on, Harvey's superiority over Marcy became evident. Isola too played better than did St. John; so that they soon made all their hoops; and Harvey got to the end first—but did not strike the stick. On the contrary he came down like a fire-ship upon his enemies, and routed the combined forces effectually. As the ball came spinning through the field again, Marcy called out, "Are you a rover, Mr. Wyndham?"

To which he answered, "Yes! that is my speciality!"

"I think it is," said Marcy laughing in her

shrill childlike way. "A rover in all things,
Mr. Wyndham! see how you have roved from
me to Mrs. Aylott! I think I will call you the
rover!" as she struck her partner's ball lightly
and carried him triumphantly through the
hoop.

A few strokes now finished the game; and
Harvey and Isola were the winners. But poor
Isola had to suffer for her vicarious victory,
for her husband, who was more annoyed than
he cared to confess, would neither speak to nor
look at her pleasantly. In a short time he
separated himself from her altogether, and went
away with Marcy, at the moment when Isola
was receiving a lesson from Harvey as to the
best mode of holding her mallet, so that she
could not accompany them. He did this intentionally, being in the mood to give himself
pain that he might revenge it on her afterwards.
We all do this kind of thing occasionally; but
Aylott St. John Aylott did it often.

"I don't think your husband liked being
beaten," said Harvey when they had gone.

Isola hesitated. She could not say he did not mind it; she would not confess that he was annoyed; and she had too little of that ready tact, got only by intercourse with society, to make, off-hand, a glib answer that would turn the conversation aside. So she looked down and said shyly, " I don't think men ever like to be beaten in games by their wives. It seems unnatural to them if they are alone, and almost traitorous when there are sides and other players."

"Especially where the games are those of skill," said Harvey. "Personal pride comes in then, as well as that more subtle sentiment of fidelity so beautifully felt and given by you."

" Oh, but I did not win this game, it was you!" she cried.

" Well, yes, of course it was, I being the older hand and the more experienced; but you certainly played better than he"—Harvey knew the full value of that familiar allusive ' he'—" and perhaps he did not like your gaining a victory by the help of an ' enemy' any more than if you had gained it by your own superior skill."

"I must not play against him again," said Isola. "There is no good in vexing one's husband for such a stupid thing as a game at croquet!"

"Has it ever struck you, Mrs. Aylott, how much stronger women are than men?" asked Harvey in his scientific voice; "how much more self-command, self-sacrifice, and patience they have?"

"We have more patience and sacrifice certainly," said Isola; "but then we are trained to them. Men have the nobler qualities, I think, but we—"

"The more angelic," he interrupted. "The ideal of a woman is an angel."

"But the archangels are men," said Isola simply; "so that even in heaven you have the highest place."

"You think we have the highest place here? I mean by that, the best place, personally and socially considered?"

"Yes," she said.

"And you envy us! Now I envy you. I

cannot say I should like to be a woman exactly, but still I envy you."

" I am sure I should not like to be a man ; and I do not envy you," laughed Isola.

" Not if you think we have the highest place?"

" No, for I should not care to have your privileges," she said.

And then she coloured. There were certain privileges of freedom and independence denied to her for which she very earnestly wished, and, had she been a man, would have inherited by right.

" Then you are unlike your sex of the present day—they are all crying out for greater freedom; and I think," said Harvey Wyndham remembering his sect, " that they ought to have it. But the truth is, the great difference between men and women lies in the difference between influence and action. You influence and we act—you are the spiritual directors and we the mechanical agents. Is it not so?"

" Not always," said Isola. " It may be true generally, but not in all individual cases, and

scarcely in all countries," she added, thinking
of Mormonism and the East, and woman's status
there.

" To come home—always a convincing line of
argument—I should say it was so in your case,"
Harvey said quite naturally, in the quietest tone
of voice possible and with the easiest and most
matter of fact manner.· " Judging of your two
characters, I should say that you carried the
heaviest metal as we riflemen say—that you had
the largest amount of power—and that you were
consequently the secret if not the open ruler of
your joint lives."

"Oh, how mistaken you are!" cried Isola
hastily.

She was surprised into the exclamation, and
the next instant she would have given worlds to
have recalled it.   She had no desire to make
Harvey Wyndham her confidant, but he was
worming himself into her secret thoughts in a
quiet irrepressible manner which she neither
understood nor could check.

"No ? How strangely one may be deceived !

Even I, an old, well-used student of life as I am,
dérouté by a young couple like yourselves, just
like the babes in the wood for innocence and
simplicity! And you have not the real influence
in your house? you are not the energizing principle? I can scarcely believe it! and yet I know
it must be true if you say so. Then Mr. Aylott
is one of those who hold the Mohammedan notion
of the inferiority and natural abasement of women? Ah well!" speaking rapidly to prevent
her replying, " if I were married, I should organize my life on a very different plan. I should
consider my wife my equal in all things, and my
superior in many. Had I a wife like you, capable, strong, sweet-tempered, devoted, I would
not make it a question of mastership; we should
be joint masters, each equally free and equally
bound—the perfect harmony of two notes, the
perfect adjustment of two spheres. That is my
idea of marriage : not mastership on either side,
but equality. What do you say, Mrs. Aylott?
Are these your views of the perfect marriage, or
are you one of the Griselda school, holding to

the natural inferiority of your sex, and consequently to their natural servitude?"

"The equal marriage seems to me the best if
it can be carried out," said Isola reluctantly.

"And that is just what so few Englishmen are
able to accord to their wives!" cried Harvey
again with his scientific voice; "either they make
them drawing-room dolls—pet birds in a gilded
cage, and nothing more—or they send them into
the fields to work for the family. Don't you
see what I mean?"

"Yes," she said.

"And both extremes are wrong."

"I think so," said Isola. "I think if a woman is worth anything, she ought to share her
husband's life and possess his confidence; but
on the other hand, she ought not to be taken out
of her sphere, either for work or authority. For
after all," earnestly, "the home is the woman's
true place!"

"Precisely what I feel," said Harvey; "and a
home in the country the ideal of its kind. Fond
as I am of the great rush and strife of London,

and liking to be in the front of the battle, fighting and toiling with the rest, I must say that I like the country for the home. Had I a wife, I should live in the country. By the by," suddenly, "has Mr. Aylott made up his mind to buy the Hermitage ?"

"I do not know if he has quite decided, but I believe he has been thinking of it," she answered.

"What price do they ask ?"

"I do not know."

"I thought, if you did, I might be of some little help, for I know something of the value of land."

He knew nothing of the kind, but he had got what he wanted—an answer which showed him that St. John did not confide in his wife nor tell her of his affairs.

"Have you any interest in business life ?" he then asked.

"I know nothing of it," she laughed.

"Not of the price of stocks ? don't you understand the value of mining shares ?"

" No !" she said good-humouredly.

" Don't you know the dividend days ? and the quotations in the share market ?"

" No !"

" Not when your husband gets a rich dividend ?"

" I do not think Mr. Aylott has any shares in anything," she answered.

" Oh yes, he has ! he has shares in a lot of things. I happen to know this, for I am joint holder as well. Did you never speculate as to the probable investment of his funds ?"

" No, never; why should I ?" she answered quickly.

" Ah well ! we are all vastly different; and I should tell my wife everything of the kind," said Harvey with a slight sigh, which made Isola more uncomfortable than all the rest had done.

Surely, surely, she was not a wife whose ill-treatment by her husband, or her unhappiness resulting, needed the sympathy of others ! Had she been foolish enough to say anything which could lead to such a false conclusion ?

"But my husband is quite right to keep things secret from me if he thinks best," she said with a little spirit, her wifely instinct overcoming her literal truth.

And Harvey read that too, and understood it and doubled down the page just in time to prevent the vague discomfort from becoming active displeasure. But he knew that he had sown the seeds of future uneasiness all the same.

By this time Marcy, who had taken St. John to see her aviary, and her new lory, and her pet fire-finches, and her great Australian crow, and all the rest of her favourite creatures, emerged from behind the tulip-tree which concealed the entrance to the winding-way leading through the shrubbery. Mr. Tremouille was with them now, and a group of strangers as well—two ladies and a gentleman, whom she introduced to Isola Aylott as "Mr. and Mrs. Joyce, our clergyman; and this is Rosa Varley, my friend."

CHAPTER X.

CONTRASTS.

MR. AND MRS. JOYCE were people of ordinary ca-
libre enough, just such people as one meets in
country places, of cleanly souls and natural lives,
but of small range of thought and of less origi-
nality of mind. He was a tall, dark-haired, florid
man inclined to indolence and obesity, and of
very moderate abilities; she, a soft, fair, weak-
eyed, and well-sized woman, of intense power of
submission and faculty of worship. She was of
the nature of a slave; a woman whose obedience
was instinctive, and to whom a husband was *ex
officio* a divinity. They were well suited in their
mutual adoration, and made quite a model

couple; but they need not have been so demonstrative as they were, and Mrs. Joyce need not have
made her own happiness so entirely the square by
which to measure the deficiences of other wives.

For it was her firm belief that all unhappy
marriages dated from the wife only ; and that to
the coldness, the independence, and the want of
the adoring faculty generally in women, were
due the sole causes of matrimonial disagree-
ment. She could not understand that fortune
had dealt generously by her in giving her precisely the kind of man for whom she was best
suited and who best suited her; and that the
legal plea of "incompatibility of temper" may
sometimes be a righteous one, and include no
blame to either side ; but she made her portion
the gauge of all others ; and because she was
rapturously content, maintained that others ought
to be rapturous likewise ; and because she and
her husband were " twin halves " happily joined,
thought that all other couples should be twin
halves too, no matter what the difference of colour, angle, or material.

She was certainly very bitter to unhappy wives. Why were they not happy? she used to say pettishly; she was happy with her Simmy, why could not others do as she did? If men were cross, it was the woman's duty to be kind; if they were a little tyrannical, women should submit; she had no patience with this new doctrine of individuality and freedom, and all such nonsense; she never did anything her Simmy did not approve of, and why should others? But she forgot to add that her Simmy never disapproved of anything she proposed; and that if she gave her tale of sugary submission, she received it back in kind, and had no draught of gall to even qualify its sweetness.

Marcy did not care much for the turtle doves, as she sometimes called them disdainfully. They were too well satisfied with themselves and with each other to afford any amusement to outsiders; and Marcy liked amusement; and above all things liked to be the centre of attraction, even with the husbands of other women. But she affected Rosa Varley, whom she called her friend

par excellence, and who came often to the Hall to
help while away the lagging hours. Rosa was a
girl of the same type as her sister—soft, yielding, large-eyed, adoring—one of the women who
weaken the moral fibre of men by their self-
abasement and submission, and who are dedi-
cated by nature to Griseldadom and slavery. She
was a susceptible girl too, and was always in
love. She had fallen desperately in love with old
Mr. Tremouille when she first came, for want of
something better; then she pined and cried about
a young doctor from the neighbouring town, who
had been called in to attend her sister; and now
she had transferred her facile yearning heart to
Harvey Wyndham, from London, though she was
not so silly as to refuse to see that her chance in
that quarter was very poor if Marcy Tremouille
chose to smile. Still, she loved; and cried about
the brisk and business-like man at night; and
made her blue eyes of a pale purple by reason of
the redness of their lids; and blushed and sighed
and simpered and looked down, and behaved like
a goose generally, as she was, and would most

probably always be. For, being a slave, she had neither pride nor self-respect, but stood in the matrimonial market with a supplicating air, feeling that she could never be sufficiently grateful to the man who might chance to take her. To her way of thinking, she and all her kind were just so many noughts, to which the commanding number alone gave any value. Harvey Wyndham, as the commanding number, would give his nought a fabulous value, she thought, raising her soft, prominent eyes to him lovingly, and hating Isola Aylott for her beauty on the one hand, and for the attention paid to her by Mr. Wyndham on the other.

After a short time spent in common-places, a new game of croquet was arranged, with four players a-side this time; and to Isola's annoyance and Rosa's intense distress, the Joyces, Harvey Wyndham, and Isola were bracketed together, while Rosa and Mr. Tremouille backed St. John and Marcy. Isola tried to change sides, but unsuccessfully; so, if she would not make a scene, saw herself forced into opposition to her husband again. And again her side won, to St. John's unconcealed mortification.

"You do well, you see, Isola, when you are my enemy," he said bitterly with a forced laugh.

"Why would you not let me be on your side?" she asked.

"I would not spoil your pleasure," he answered with a sneer.

"I make a point of never playing against *my* husband," said Mrs. Joyce emphatically.

"Ah! but you see my wife is a strong-minded person, and likes to show her independence," said St. John, with perfect breeding, but with an unpleasant expression of face.

"I had nothing to do with the arrangement of the game. I would willingly have played on the other side," said Isola very much disturbed.

She felt the tone of rebuke in which Mrs. Joyce spoke as specially unjust, and perhaps she answered with just a shade more earnestness than she need have done.

"I would have insisted, if I had been you," said the clergyman's wife, with a little laugh that was meant to disguise the rather bitter spirit in her words. "I do not care what I do to any one so long as I keep with my husband."

"Oh, but Mrs. Aylott belonged to Mr. Wyndham," said Marcy as if making a diversion in Iola's favour. "Mr. Wyndham the rover!" she added with a most peculiar accent.

"Don't, Miss Tremouille!" said Mrs. Joyce severely. "It is not pleasant to hear such things said."

"My goodness, what have I said!" cried Marcy with prettily-acted surprise.

"What is always very painful to me to hear—coupled the name of a married woman with that of an unmarried man," said Mrs. Joyce.

Isola stood with burning cheeks; St. John was of a dull leaden hue.

"This is rather an unfortunate discussion," he said with a forced smile. "I do not exactly understand how it has arisen."

"Not fairly," said Isola in a low voice, but distinctly too.

"It only shows the great need that married

women have of caution," observed Mr. Joyce demurely.

"I do not see where I was incautious," said Isola.

Mrs. Joyce smiled unpleasantly. Marcy had already given her a disagreeble impression of Mrs. Aylott, and having a stronger sense of her duties as a clergyman's wife than she had of those as a gentlewoman, she was resolved to set the new comer at the Hermitage in the straight path, if so be she could first find out wherein she wandered.

"Well, I cannot understand what it is all about!" cried Marcy; "so come, Rosa dear, let us go away together and leave all those funny quarrelsome people to themselves. My goodness, Rosa, what a goose your sister is!" she said as soon as they were out of hearing. "Poor Mrs. Aylott! she is in for it now! But I think she deserves it too. I think she is one of your quiet flirts who make men in love with them, and then say they didn't know. And if there is one thing I hate more than another, it is a flirting wife!" said Marcy Tremouille energetically.

"So do I," echoed Rosa, looking hard at
Harvey Wyndham, who, under the guise of col-
lecting the hoops and balls, had the air of not
having heard what had been passing.

As Marcy went away Isola turned aside too,
hoping that St. John would follow her; but instead of that, he joined Rosa Varley and Marcy
Tremouille, where they stood apart whispering
and laughing together, and soon after sauntered with them through the shrubbery, while the
Joyces went into the arbour under the tulip-tree.
Mr. Tremouille had left the ground before the discussion arose.

Then Harvey went up to Isola, standing alone
and apparently absorbed in contemplating an
agapanthos, and Mrs. Joyce said to her husband,
"Well! if this is not flirting, Simmy, I should
like to know what is! I am sure I don't wonder
at Mr. Aylott being annoyed—such new comers
and everything—but what a dreadful creature
she must be! and that bold horrid Mr. Wyndham! He is just one of those bold bad London
men who are the very pests of society. I am sure
h e is!"

And the Reverend Simeon answered, "I do not like the looks of him," uneasily, unconsciously pressing his wife's hand more closely within his arm, as if she too might be in danger: in which she was not.

"I am so sorry Mr. Aylott is so much annoyed!" said Harvey sympathetically. "Croquet shows the temper more than anything else I know of. I can read a whole field after a game or two. Now your husband is jealous and arbitrary, and likes to be the dominant power, and foremost in all things."

"I will not play again," said Isola, unconsciously allowing all that Harvey had surmised.

"Nonsense, Mrs. Aylott! that is childish. Let me advise you—I have been the witness of a small unpleasantness for a very silly cause—but let me advise you to keep your ground. If you yield up your right of individuality in these little things, you will have to give up others more serious and important. A woman has rights of action, remember, married or single; and no laws can touch her freedom within the limits of her own sphere."

So for the second time Isola was taught the doctrine of individuality, and independence of her husband's will. The words burnt a little, and caused a certain vague trouble in her soul; and yet they did not seem to her as true as when Jane had said them, nor spoken from so high a platform.

As they walked home together, late in the afternoon, Isola wanted to make friends again, as children say, but St. John was so cool in manner and curt in speech, though also, as always, formally polite, that the poor girl could do nothing. She was paralysed and helpless. He kept his head turned resolutely away, save when he spoke, and then he bent it with excessive courtesy—but he spoke with his teeth shut and his lips drawn close to a point; he answered her with mathematical precision, but he only answered her. And yet she could not complain. He was quite blameless in all he said and did, and she had not the faintest opportunity for a remonstrance or a quarrel, nor even for an explanation. It was simply the excessive ceremoniousness which oppressed her more than any amount of loud rebuke would have done. But it was St. John's way of showing displeasure, and she had to accept it and make the best of it; and having a sweet temper, she did make the best of it, and let it pass unnoticed. Perhaps St. John would have been better pleased had she burst into tears or blazed up into a fit of anger. The first would have humiliated her, the last would have put her in the wrong; and either way would have given him the higher place, and have afforded him an excuse for a grave and commanding rebuke. So they walked on in an uncomfortable fashion enough, till they came to Buckhurst Ground and the three cottages within the sweep.

Sitting on a settle by the door where Mr. Tremouille had spoken to Nancy Wilson, was an old man, grey, withered, and feeble, basking there in the sun, as if to get back into his shrivelled veins some of the leaping fire and warmth of his lustier years. But withered and old and wan as he was, there was something in his face so beautiful—there was an expression of such divine patience—of sorrow which had become sanctification—and of a spiritual life rising higher than the social and physical abasement of this earthly one—that Isola involuntarily stopped, and bent her head with a smiling, friendly greeting, saying "Good day" as she came up. She was astonished at herself for doing so; but the impulse was stronger than habit, and she broke through the usual shy reserve of her life, almost as if she had been bidden to do so.

"Good day, ma'am; it's a fine day," said the old man in a voice singularly sweet for one of the class used to wet, and exposure, and drunken ale-house songs, and hoarse field cries, and all the other things which tarnish the silver of the throat and make it into rusty iron instead.

"Have you been ill?" asked Isola, leaving her husband's side to go nearer to the old man. "You look ill."

"Yes, what I've been a little bit dashed of late," he answered with a smile.

"What has been the matter with you?" she asked.

" Well, I think it's just old age, ma'am. I'm seventy-four last birthday, and that's a good time of life. I've nothing particular to speak of. The cough's bad at nights, and I've no great spirit for my meat; but I'm better again now, thank God; and maybe I'll round the bad end of the year, and see another lambing time."

" Have you all you ought to have ?" said Isola. " Cannot we send you something from the Hermitage ?"

" Thank you kindly, ma'am, I'm sure, but I want for nothing. They's very good to me at the Hall, and don't let me want."

" But we might help too," said Isola.

" Well, thank you, there's nothing I've a mind for, but it's kindness in you all the same. You like the Hermitage, sir, I understand ?" he then said, addressing St. John rather suddenly.

"Yes, very well on the whole," St. John answered haughtily. He was not fond of poor people.

" I'm glad of that !—for many's the year I've worked on them grounds," said the old man with a gentle smile; "I was on them for more nor forty years, man and boy; all through Mrs. Archer Holmes's time and before. But I left when madam died; and master Gilbert he sold off and went to California, and the place got into new hands. I went up to the Hall then, and they took me on there, and there I've been eighteen year come Michaelmas—ever since Miss Marcy was born. I mind I went the week before, and never saw the lady at all, for she died with little Miss a-coming."

"Do you want to hear any more, Isola?" asked St. John disdainfully.

He was standing with his back to the sunlight and his hat pressed over his eyes, as he always wore it, so that his face could not be seen, but Isola knew by his voice and attitude that he was annoyed and wished to get away. Going up to him she said in a low voice, "Dear St. John, give me some money—give me half-a-sovereign for him."

The old man overheard her.

"Thank you kindly, ma'am," he said eagerly

with a slight flush on his cheek; "you've no call to do it. I want for nothing; our master takes care of that."

"But I should like to give you something whether you want it or not," said Isola ingenuously.

"You've no call," repeated the old man holding out his hand; and the gesture said that the hand-press of human sympathy and equality was worth all the guineas ever coined. "I'll be main pleased to see you whenever you be passing this way, but you've no occasion to give me nought."

Isola laid her kind hand in his and clasped her fingers over his broad and shrivelled palm with a frank pressure.

He lifted his face to hers with a kind of reverent admiration.

"Thank you," he said; "that does me more good nor money."

Then he held out his hand to St. John and said, "And I'll be glad to see you too, sir, when you may be passing this way again, and hoping to see you main soon," very cordially, but more

as if giving an invitation to an equal than as if
praying for a grace from a superior.

This seemed to St. John as almost the ultimate
degree to which impertinent familiarity could be
carried. He had not yet got to the knowledge
that the peasantry consider their cottages as
houses, and their houses as homes of which they
are the masters both to bar and to invite. To
him they were all just so many half-brutish serfs,
who ought to feel it an overwhelming honour if a
superior condescended to recognize their human
existence at all. But because he was a gentleman, and understood that gentlehood has its obligations, he went up to the old peasant, and laid
his well-fitting gloved hand in the horny hand
held out to him. As he came nearer the old man
gave a start.

" Hey, what's this !" he said, shading his brow
with his hand.

" Is my husband like any one you know ?"
Isola asked.

He drew a deep breath. " Like ?" he repeated
as if a little bewildered, " No, no one I know,

ma'am. It was just a daze for a moment. No! like no one."

"I should not think it very likely that I could resemble any of your friends!" said St. John very haughtily. Then laying a sovereign on the bench beside him, he said coldly, "There! that is something more to the purpose—and what you will understand."

The old man looked pained. "It would be thankless to say no, sir," he said in a low voice, "and I thank you for your kindness all the same, but I'd rather you'd not have done it. We poor men do not like to be always paid with money—a kind word from a gentleman sometimes goes further than money!"

"I think you will have to take what gentlemen choose to give!" said St. John Aylott moving away. "Come, Isola, if you are ready—I am waiting."

"I will come and see you again," said Isola very kindly. With her keener sympathies she had comprehended the whole situation. "And, remember, if we can do anything for you at the Hermitage, you must let us know. By the by," suddenly, "what is your name?"

" Aaron Wilson, ma'am; grandfather to my Nancy as you spoke to t'other evening when you was along with the squire."

" I have only one favour to beg of you, my dear Isola," said St. John stiffly, before they were well out of hearing. " I do not seek to interfere with you, understand, or to direct you against your will, but I beg that you will not force me to join you in what I disapprove. Another time I will publicly refuse you; which will not be pleasant to your feelings, I imagine."

" What have I done to vex you ?" asked Isola a little timidly.

" You have vexed me by many things, Isola— by your familiarity of manner to Mr. Wyndham, which, I confess, as much astonished as it vexed me; by your gross familiarity to this old boor; and by your presuming to ask me for money before him. Am I a child, or your servant, that you should dictate to me what I am to do? How dare you use such a freedom to me, Isola? If you ever do it again, I tell you I will refuse you before the whole world."

He spoke vehemently, almost wildly, but with a deepened lowered voice, as if his passion was concentrating rather than effervescing.

"But what am I to do?" asked Isola. "I have no money of my own—what can I do when I wish to give anything away?"

"It is no business of mine what you are to do," said St. John. "I only know what I will not allow to be done to me."

"But every one has something of their own," urged Isola, and she was surprised at her own insistance. "Miss Tremouille—my poor mother —every woman I know anything about has money to spend as she likes! If I may neither have it nor ask you to do what I want, what can I do?"

"You have dropped the mask rather soon, Isola!" the husband said with an angry gesture and a bitter sneer.

"I do not understand you, St. John! I have not understood you of late at all," she answered warmly. "You treat me as if I had done something really wrong—you say cruel things—you are quite changed to me—always cold, always displeased—and why? Only tell me what I have done! Let me know my fault at least! I cannot mend things if I do not know where I have offended!"

"You are offending me now," said St. John coldly. "And I think, my dear Isola, if you will moderate your voice a little it will be better—do you want the Newfield peasantry to hear Mr. and Mrs. Aylott disputing like themselves?"

"St. John, you are unjust!" said Isola in a deep voice.

He bowed. "I must accept your decision," he said with an ironical smile. "Perhaps Mr. Wyndham will prove a more equitable judge."

"For shame!" said Isola with crimson cheeks, and turned away from him angrily.

That evening St. John wrote to London for a croquet set, but he did not tell Isola that he had done so; neither did he consult with her, nor ask her to accompany him when he went into the garden after dinner, and measured out the exact plot of lawn that was to serve as the ground.

Things had begun to assume the shape of division in his mind, and henceforth his life and hers— his pleasures and hers—was no longer identical as before. He could not understand any separate individual action as consistent with a true marriage, and Isola had unwittingly snapped asunder some of the finest threads and broken some of the tenderer links.

The next morning he drew out his cheque-book, and wrote a cheque for fifty pounds, made payable to Isola's order.

"You had a hundred a year, Isola, when you came of age," he said in a hard dry voice. "There were no settlements; I do not think that any man who respects himself would suffer settlements to be made on his marriage, and no woman who loved or respected her husband would desire them; but since you have resolved on taking your own way independent of me, here is the first half-year's payment of your allowance."

"Dearest St. John," said Isola with tears in her eyes, "I don't wish this! I only want to have a little money for charities and things of that kind. It seems throwing me off to give me my own money independently like this! as if you were seriously offended with me!"

"It does not much matter to you whether I am offended or not," said St. John as coldly as before. "You have your own way, and that is generally enough for most women!"

"Not enough for me if you are vexed with me," she said.

"Pshaw!" said St. John Aylott. "I am afraid, Isola, you think me more easily imposed on than I am."

"Easily imposed on! do I want to impose on you, St. John?"

"My dear child," he answered in the most philosophic manner of assured superiority, a manner which had always grated on Isola and which now was specially hard to bear, "you are a woman, and as such arbitrary and un-just. You demand to have everything your own way. For instance—to prove it to yourself—you want to be independent of me, but only just to the extent and in the manner you desire; you want to do as you like, without reference to my wishes; and you are not content with the liberty to do as you like, but you wish to force me into a line of action distinctly opposed to my own wishes and principles. This is what I call unjust and arbitrary, and what I must positively decline to submit to. And because I will not submit to it, but simply exercise the same amount of freedom as you demand for yourself, you think yourself ill-used. This is folly, my dear Isola, and shows a worse temper and a more selfish disposition than I once believed it possible for you to show. You must conquer these little failings, my dear child, and you must understand that you cannot have everything; and that if you take your own way, you must be content with this, and not expect to govern me also, nor to have my approbation. Now we will drop the subject. You have your first half-yearly instalment in your hands, and you are independent of your husband; but when the consequences of your own act come, do not blame me for them."

And with the same strange glare in his eyes
and the same unpleasant smile about his lips
that Isola had seen in him once before, he left
the room hurriedly, and she saw no more of him
till dinner-time.

When he came back he was flushed and excited, but no more friendly than before; a little
loud and boisterous in manner, and a little insolent and mocking as well—assuming at every turn
that he was nothing now to Isola, and that she had
discarded him and all interest in his concerns.

When she asked him where he had been? he
only answered with a painful laugh, " And how
can that possibly interest you, Isola ? What do
you care now for me, where I go or what I do ?
If you do not care to know for love, I will not be
questioned for interference !" he added with a
sudden outburst of anger.

She learnt afterwards from Marcy that he
had been at the Hall, playing croquet with the
party there; "and so happy, so delightful!" said
Marcy enthusiastically and with extreme simplicity of accent—but she looked at Isola while she

spoke; "not a bit like what he was the first day!"

"I am glad he was so happy," said Isola; and Marcy's sleepy eyes searched her face in vain. She was too large for the smallness of jealousy, too noble for the degradation of suspicion; and if she felt hurt that she had been intentionally excluded from participation in her husband's pleasure, she had the courage and the strength to conceal her pain.

"She is a block!" thought Marcy, "but I'll make her jealous yet!"

CHAPTER XI.

SHADOWS.

THE intimacy between the Hall and the Hermitage grew daily, though with a certain unacknowledged reserve on Isola's part, a certain feeling of disquiet with Harvey and of constraint with Marcy, that somewhat marred her pleasure in their new friends. Left to herself she would not have been so intimate; but it was St. John's doing; and he who had never willingly left his wife for half an hour, nor gone into a friend's house, nor admitted a friend into his, was now never happy but when he was lounging away his days at the Hall, flirting with Marcy Tremouille, and studying "life" at the feet of Harvey Wynd-

ham. And he did flirt with Marcy, and Marcy
flirted with him.

This entanglement of married men was Marcy's
grand employment and recreation. Determined
on a good marriage, if any, yet unable to resist
the coquettish instincts that seemed to have been
given her, just to show how lovely she would
have been had she had truth or heart, she was as
wary with the unmarried as she was dangerous
with the married. She had no desire to be
mixed up with unprofitable love affairs that
would have necessitated explanations, and perhaps the removal of cherished masks; but married men were so safe, she used to say. They
could not ask her to run away with them, or to
marry them; and she could play off all her pretty
tricks without fearing the day of reckoning and
retribution. And if she made the wives jealous,
that was their fault, not hers, stupid things!
What did she do but talk and laugh and be
complaisant and submissive, as a woman should
be? Was a man to be a mere bear because he
had a wife, and was he to be afraid of speaking

to any other woman? If St. John Aylott, for instance, liked to be with her better than with his own wife, who was to blame but Isola herself? She should flatter and study him as she, Marcy, did, and not leave it to an outsider to make her husband happy in his own way.

So she said—omitting the reference to herself —when Mrs. Joyce was discussing with her the condition of the "young people;" and Mrs. Joyce, who, as we know, could not tolerate anything like character in wives, agreed with her warmly, and told the Reverend Simeon afterwards that Marcy had some very proper notions about things, but that she feared this new comer at the Hermitage, this handsome Mrs. Aylott, was not quite as wifely as she should be. Marcy, who saw a good deal of them, said as much, and poor dear Mr. Aylott certainly did not look very happy.

"Perhaps," concluded Mrs. Joyce with a reflective air, "Marcy may have a good influence over Mrs. Aylott, and cause her to see her duty better."

"She should come to you, Bessie, to know

what a good wife is," said Mrs. Joyce pulling a flaxen ringlet with clumsy playfulness.

"But then I have such a husband!" said Mrs. Joyce fondly.

And then they expatiated on their mutual perfections till tea-time came.

Hitherto this peculiar propensity of Marcy's had escaped much notice. Her father's position and her own wonderful simplicity of manner had preserved her name intact, and kept the current of gossip, always flowing in country places, very low indeed. To be sure, one or two little indiscretions had been noticed; but people are chary of saying evil of a young and beautiful girl, motherless, and the daughter of a magnate; and the wide cloak of charity had been thrown over her, with no stint in the folds. And after all, she reasoned—and the world good-naturedly reasoned for her—she did nothing that was really wrong, so she ought not to be condemned. She used to be more caressing and familiar with her rare male acquaintances than was wise, truly; but that was all; and want of wisdom is not want of

grace. So she flirted with St. John as she had
flirted with his predecessor Mr. Sutherland, who
had rented the Hermitage before him ; and if
Isola did not like it, that was her own affair, said
Marcy ; she ought to learn to bear what she
didn't like, and to do disagreeable things gracefully—at least Miss Walsh, her governess, had
always said so to her ; and what was good for her
was good for Isola.

That she was undermining the young wife's
happiness never crossed Marcy's mind with pity
or compunction. That St. John went home irritated against her for her mere upright truthfulness, contrasted with the supple flattery so
liberally dealt out to him at the Hall, was to
her a matter of supreme indifference. She had
had her amusement through the long warm summer day, and it was no business of hers what
price others had to pay at the end of it. It was
very dull at Newfield, and St. John and Harvey
together could not make life inordinately exciting to her ; and as "bad is the best" thought
Marcy, she did not scruple to take that best

freely. But Isola remained at home alone, and
wondered ; scarcely able to understand what
manner of shadow it was that was slowly gathering over her life, and blotting out all the sunshine
thereof.

One day Marcy drove over to the Hermitage,
her lovely face radiant with pleasure.

" Why, what has made you so specially bright
to-day ?" said Isola smiling.

"I am so delighted ! " cried Marcy.

" What is it ? Has your cousin come ? the one
you have been expecting so long ? Mr. Holmes ?"
asked Isola. For the girl had confided to her
how anxiously she was looking for the arrival of
this cousin.

" No, it is not that," said Marcy shaking her
head with her pretty assumption of childishness.
" Cousin Gilbert came yesterday, but that is not
what has pleased me so much."

" And yet you have been wishing him to come
so often," said Isola.

" Oh yes, and so I am very glad that he has
come, very glad indeed !" raising her sleepy eyes.

"But it is something much nicer than cousin Gilbert's coming that has made me so happy. Fancy, Isola dear, my darling little lory has laid the sweetest little eggs you can imagine, and wants to sit! I can't tell you how glad I am!—a cage full of little darlings, all out of my own eggs!"

When she spoke she looked up into Isola's face with a strange expression—strange at least for her theme. It was the expression of one watching, almost asking. Yet why should she watch? what should she ask?

Isola smiled a little sadly. There was an accent of untruth and pretence in the girl's voice which struck upon her heart, and made her feel uncertain, and, what was so rare for her, suspicious.

As Marcy stood there by the table, her face turned smiling to Isola, the lovely curves of her figure well expressed, and the languid grace peculiar to her a little more languid and a great deal more graceful than was even usual, she was a picture unmatched for beauty. The sun was

streaming into the room, and fell across the girl,
bringing out every line and tint with redoubled
brilliancy, while leaving Isola in comparative
shadow. But how much nobler was the fair face
looking into Marcy's sleepy, languid, darker
beauty! The steadfast deep blue eyes, so tender
and so frank; the generous lips smiling too, but
lightly closed; the bended forehead full of character and power; the look of womanly sweetness and force so peculiarly Isola's own—what a
far nobler face it was, and what a much more
heroic and capable nature it indicated! Beautiful as Marcy was, there was something in Isola
that faded and impoverished her—something that
showed where the want lay—something that em-
bittered Marcy's very soul with jealousy, and
that, all unknown to Isola and scarcely confessed to herself, made her the young wife's
secret and determined enemy.

"Have you seen my husband to-day?" then
asked Isola.

This was the newest phase of St. John's displeasure with his wife; he regulated his life on

the strictest principles of secrecy, and hid his
goings and his comings from her as if he had
been a conspirator billeted with a spy. He was
one of those extreme souls who never do things
by halves. When he was displeased he was at
deadly war, and if everything was not entirely
sympathetic there was nothing that remained
harmonious.

"Yes, he was at our house when I came
away, I think," said Marcy. He had handed
her into the carriage. "He and papa and
cousin Gilbert were all together, I believe. Oh!
and they said I was to tell you that they were
coming here to luncheon. I am to stay till they
come, and then we are all to walk home by the
lane, and you are to dine with us and spend the
evening. I remember it all now, but I was
so enchanted about my dear little lory that I
forgot."

"Naughty girl!" laughed Isola.

"Yes, am I not? But you see I don't care
for Harvey Wyndham so much," was Marcy's
somewhat inexplicable answer.

And Isola stared. She often missed the point of Marcy Tremouille's sly attacks; her mind not being much awake to this kind of covert wounding.

As the two young creatures stood there, a hum of male voices was heard at a little dis-tance. And presently came one nearer and alone, a rich, sonorous, manly voice, saying, "Ah! there is the dear old place again, not much changed in all these years! My dear mother's window—my father's room—just the same as ever!"

The instant after, the low French window opening on to the lawn was darkened, and St. John Aylott passed through into the drawing-room, followed by Gilbert Holmes, Massinger's residuary legatee and Marcy Tremouille's cousin. Mr. Tremouille and Harvey Wyndham were be-hind, and did not enter quite at the same mo-ment.

"Mr. Holmes, Isola," said St. John curtly, and Isola went through the prescribed cere-monial of an introduction. But Gilbert Holmes, as if not content with the formal bow which merely acknowledged his existence, went straight up to her and shook hands, as one who had the right by long association if not by early knowledge—looking into her face frankly and pleasantly.

It was strange how much they were alike in type, and how different to the rest. They might have been brother and sister for likeness of general expression, not coming quite so close as likeness of feature. It was easy for an ethnologist to see that they both belonged to the fair-haired, strong-limbed Scandinavian race, whereas St. John had as evidently southern blood in him, Mr. Tremouille and Harvey were Celts, and Marcy was the daughter of a quadroon. And they met more like old friends long parted and as yet only doubtfully recognizing each other, or like compatriots in a foreign land, than as utter strangers with no lines of relation woven even in imagination between them.

Marcy watched that meeting more keenly than

did even St. John; she gathered every word and look and fleeting colour into her heart, as a cup gathers slowly poison drop by drop. She had disliked Isola from the first, and from the first had been jealous of her power and beauty, but she had never hated her as she did now, and had never known the strength of jealousy as she knew it now. If she could have struck her blind —disfigured—dead—as she stood there talking to Gilbert Holmes—he smiling down into her face as if he had found something he loved to look at—she would have done so; but she only lisped a good deal, and caressed her very sweetly, and once turning to St. John, said softly, "How pretty your wife looks when she is animated! and how animated she is looking now! I wonder what cousin Gilbert is saying to her—and they say he is such an awful flirt!"

Following out the programme as promulgated by Marcy, when luncheon was over they all went out together to walk to the Hall by way of the lane and Buckhurst Ground. It was a soft grey summer day, clouded and sunless, so that even Marcy could walk that leafy mile in comfort, and not declare herself ready to die more than half-a-dozen times in the transit.

At first they all kept well together, but after a time Isola found herself alone with Gilbert, having distanced the rest. They talked of many things, but chiefly of California and the life there; and Gilbert told some anecdotes of grisly bears and Comanche Indians, of forest fires and river snags, of dangers from the wild cattle of the prairies, and from the Indians lurking unseen in the sea of grass, or winding snakelike through the low brushwood of the cleared spaces. He told his stories well, without bravado or exaggeration, but with force too and always with point; and Isola listened with rapt interest, as Desdemona once listened to the Moor.

She had never felt for any one as she felt now for this stranger, this Gilbert Holmes. It was the instinctive reliance of the weaker on something stronger and wiser than itself—the recognition of a king of men—of a captain born to direct the feebler brethren—of her superior, and who might be her teacher. Jane Osborn was strong, yet she somehow missed the central truth; Harvey Wyndham was superficial and untrustworthy; St. John was narrow and arbitrary; but Gilbert was broad and generous and strong, yet tender too— he was the brother to the sister, the one sole person she had yet seen whom she instinctively felt would be her friend. He would stand between her and Harvey Wyndham's insidious questionings, and he would bring back St. John to a more natural and healthy state. "When we know him better, Mr. Holmes will have a good influence over him," thought Isola; and in that thought gave Gilbert her unspoken confidence.

"Shall I be taking a liberty with you, Mrs. Aylott, if I ask you to let me look up old Aaron Wilson as we pass?" asked Gilbert as they walked along the lane.

"Not the least. I should like to go with you if I may," she answered; "I often call on him, I like him so much! he seems to be such a good old man!"

" He used to be," said Gilbert; "and so patient!—the truest exemplification of the Christian serf I have ever seen. A man bearing his badge of slavery with a kind of proud humility as a burden laid on him to bear, but always patient, always humble, and manly in his very humility."

"I like that," said Isola in a low voice, just as they got to Aaron Wilson's door.

" Ah! but it's good to see you," cried the old man, as Gilbert strode into the cottage; " I never thought I'd have lived to see you again, master Gilbert, and you so far away and me so up in years. And glad to see you too, ma'am," to Isola, holding out his hand, " it's long since I saw your bonny face, ma'am."

" Well, Aaron, I'm glad to see you too, though you are not quite the man you used to be, hey?" said Gilbert pleasantly.

" Nay, nay! I'm not quite the same man as I were when you was a young 'un, master Gilbert, and we mastered the bay mare between us and set the traps o' nights. But what! we must all have our time, and mine has been a long 'un and a good 'un too, while it lasted."

"You were always cheerful and content, Aaron."

"What's the vally of aught else, master Gilbert? I've had my share of troubles, but I never misbelieved in God through it all. I knew that He had sent me what was best for me, and if I had trouble to go through it was because I had earned it. We are all tried by fire, master Gilbert, and I reckon you have had a mort of troubles in your time too."

"Yes, I have had difficulties, but I have fought through them you see," Gilbert answered cheerily.

"And it has been a terrible wild life, I'll engage?"

"Yes! wild and rough enough, Aaron—what would just have suited you when you were a youngster."

"Aye! I've always repented that chance," said Aaron with an altered face. "It may have been that it was the finger of Providence showing me the right road to go, and that what I've had since has been punishment for it."

"You mean when you had that offer to go to Monte Video?"

He nodded.

"It might have been better for you," said Gilbert gravely.

"Aye! he sighed," it might have saved all that comed afterwards. However, it ain't of no use looking back now; master Gilbert. If I've sinned, I've been punished. God 'll not take it out of me both ways. There's justice and there's mercy, else we'd be in a queer boat at the end. Here, Nancy! Nancy!" he called, "give a chair to the gentleman. You'll not remember Nancy, master Gilbert?"

Nancy came forward and set the chairs for the quality; and again Isola was struck with something in her face like some one she could not remember seen before. Gilbert too was vaguely reminded of some one, but he thought it was her former self.

"I think I should have passed Nancy," he

said, "and yet I do not know. Her face comes
back to me now."

"Aye, but seventeen year makes a vast difference between a young lass and a woman turned
of thirty," said Aaron. "Nancy was only fifteen
when you went away, master Gilbert; ye're thirty-
two now, my girl, arn't ye?"

"Yes, grandfather," said Nancy.

"That makes all the odds, ye see, master Gilbert? And the little miss ye left as a babe in
the cradle?"

"Miss Tremouille? oh, of course she is quite
a stranger," laughed Gilbert.

"Aye, needs be; and pretty is she—rare pretty;
but," sinking his voice, "not so pretty as my lass,
nor as her mother before her."

"I don't remember your daughter," said Gilbert, also in a slightly lowered voice.

"Nay, not like. She was dead before you
could remember. Let me see—you are thirty-
eight, master Gilbert, bain't you?"

"Yes," he answered. "I was twenty-one when
I left England, and I have been away seventeen
years."

"And my daughter's been dead thirty-two years come the third of December next," said Aaron. "She died when Nancy here was eight months old, and we took the child and reared it. Yes, my Honor died on the third of December thirty-two years ago, and her mother followed her two months after."

Honor Wilson! The name for the first time struck Gilbert's memory—the name of the legatee in his uncle Massinger's will, and the mother, as Richard Norton hinted, of Mrs. Harriet Grant. But Mrs. Grant was not over twenty-seven at the most, if so much. She had married early—ten years ago, at seventeen according to her own account—and she had had a hard and anxious life; but even with all these unfavourable influences, she did not look over twenty-seven at the outside. How then could she be Honor Wilson's daughter? that is, if Honor, as old Aaron said, had died eight months after the birth of Nancy?

He remembered hearing the story of the beautiful cottage-girl often spoken of, how she had sud-

denly disappeared, no one knew how or where, but
was at last traced to London, where she was found
to be living an evil life among artists and the like.
So at least said report, but no particulars were
ever heard. In due time came a little child to
the cottage, and Honor Wilson, the prettiest girl
of the village, was reported dead, and by degrees
the sad story came to be forgotten. Aaron's
wife, a Spanish woman who had been nurse at
the old Tremouilles', died soon after, and Aaron
brought up the little one with a mother's care.

Gilbert remembered all this now; and coupled
with his uncle Massinger's bequest it came back
to him as a history made suddenly clear in its
sinfulness and sorrow. Was, then, that uncle of
his the cause of the poor girl's ruin? was Nancy
his cousin by blood? was she his uncle's child?
And Mrs. Grant—that poor down-trodden creature—was she his cousin too? Thinking this,
he raised his eyes to Nancy, and the secret of her
likeness was discovered. It was Mrs. Grant of
whom she had so vaguely reminded him; and yet
not wholly. There was another point of resem-

blance left to the side which did not fit in with
the emigrant's widow—he had seen some one
else beside Harriet Grant to whom Nancy Wilson
bore the ineffaceable stamp of blood-relationship.
But at the moment he could not remember who
it was, and the vague thought passed away.

That night he wrote to Richard Norton, to tell
him how he had forgotten all about the Honor
Wilson of Newfield when speaking with him
about the legacy. He had never known the girl,
and the mere likeness of name escaped him, he
said. But connecting all things together, he
thought it likely that this Nancy was Massinger's
child as well as Honor Wilson's. But Mrs.
Grant, to whom Mr. Norton had alluded as probably interested in the legacy—was she his
uncle's daughter also? But no! that could not
be. He remembered now, her own account of
herself, at least her husband's account of her,
was quite different. How could she be Honor
Wilson's heir at all? Her father, old Aaron,
said that his daughter had died thirty-two years
ago—eight months after the birth of Nancy; was

that a real death, or only one reported? Had she made herself dead to her parents, or had they buried her in sign of repudiation? If the last, she might be living now, and in misery. Uncle Massinger used to come down to Newfield in the early days; he had often heard it spoken of at home, how he suddenly dropped all intercourse with his family, though there had been no dis-agreement among them. Was that remorse or fear? He sent these hasty thoughts to Mr. Nor-ton for his consideration; he might find in them a clue for the discovery of the truth. If he thought he could do so, he begged him to spare neither labour nor expense in the search. He should like to do justice to his uncle's memory, said Gilbert, and to repair his wrong, if it was possible.

Richard Norton smiled when he read that letter, which he docketed and put away. It amused him that Gilbert Holmes should send him "clues" for threading the dark labyrinth wherein lay the secret of Honor Wilson's true fate, and the identification of her children. But he respected the honesty of the intention; which was all that could be expected from a cynical old Voltairean

...sed in the chicanery of law, and taking huma-

PRINTED BY J. E. TAYLOR AND CO.,
LITTLE QUEEN STREET LINCOLN'S INN FIELDS.